Iron Duke

Iron Duke

JOHN R. TUNIS

With an Introduction by Bruce Brooks

An Odyssey Classic
Harcourt Brace Jovanovich, Publishers
San Diego   New York   London

HBJ

Library of Congress Cataloging-in-Publication Data
Tunis, John Roberts, 1889–
Iron duke/by John R. Tunis;
with an introduction by Bruce Brooks.
p.   cm.
"An Odyssey classic."
Summary: Entering Harvard, Jim Wellington finds himself in a
completely different world from his small hometown and gains poise
and a sense of proportion as he faces the difficulties and
disappointments of college life.
ISBN 0-15-238987-3 (pbk.)
[1. Universities and colleges — Fiction.
2. Track and field — Fiction.] I. Title.
PZ7.T8236
[Ir   1990]
[Fic] — dc20   89-24508

Printed in the United States of America
A B C D E

Introduction

One of the great things about John R. Tunis's Brooklyn Dodger novels is that although they are dated, they do not merely evoke fond nostalgia or bored contempt for the Olden Days. From page one of *The Kid from Tomkinsville* through all of its sequels, we could never mistake the world described therein for today's professional baseball scene. Yet we do not find ourselves either scoffing at the old-timers or lionizing them. Instead, we enjoy the vintage flavor for itself, and we discover under its surface a lot that is, if not hip, at least brightly contemporary.

Well, college, like baseball, ain't exactly what it used to be, either, and Tunis's two Harvard novels—

Iron Duke and *The Duke Decides*—present university life in a similarly dated yet incisive way. The
world of these two novels differs wildly (or, perhaps,
placidly) from most campus life today (even that of
proudly timeless Harvard); the absence of music,
drugs, sex, inflammatory and superficial politics,
and overriding fiscal ambition make Tunis's ivied
academe seem quaint and rather naive. Imagine—
the guys in the hero's dorm in *Iron Duke* think it's
a major prank to climb a bell tower! Hey, they really
know how to have a good time, don't they?

It may be easy at first for readers of this book to
greet the story of young Jim Wellington's arrival at
Harvard with a condescending chuckle, much the
way some East Coast snobs in the novel greet the
native of Waterloo, Iowa, with his corny earnestness
and determination. But, as usual, Tunis has set a
trap for a lazy reader ready to follow his or her
prejudices instead of the text. *Iron Duke*, without
flinching from its straightforward bildungsroman
structure, turns into a strong, serious, fun book, just
as Jim—without flinching from his own rectitude—
shows all of Harvard how a star can be slowly re-
vealed, rather than simply born.

The story, though basically simple, reflects the
twisting dazzle that can turn a teenager's head every
which way as he arrives full of hope and apprehen-

sion and finds both feelings justified in the shifting adventures of freshman life. Jim, the pride of his town on the sports field and in the classroom, comes to Harvard with a good head and an intuitive heart, devoted to the idea of making his parents proud and showing them and his Iowa friends that he was not aiming too high when he decided to come east for the best education available.

Tunis shows Jim—and us—a quick swirl of fascinating places, people, and challenges. We meet Jim's odd housemates, Mickey, a cryptic, shrewd fellow who is equal parts street tough and philosopher, and Fog, a fine guy who ignores all his opportunities to be a revered Rich Kid. We are swept unwitting into a campus riot that starts as a lark and turns into trouble; we take some heavy hits in the surprisingly tough football tryouts; we scratch our heads over difficult homework; we wend our way through a series of quirky decisions that land us first on the track team and, eventually, into several fantastic mile races against Ivy League champions. One thing leads to another, and Tunis manages to carry the reader right along with Jim in all his innocence and excitement.

As the book goes on, however, a difference grows between our perspective and Jim's. While he is observing the events of his life at Harvard with both eyes, we begin to notice we are keeping one eye firmly on him. For he is changing, growing in subtle ways into a very strong character, commanding more and more of our attention and respect. Tunis does not break the unself-conscious nature of Jim's point of view to offer a commentary that illuminates Jim's growth; he trusts us to notice it on our own—just as, finally, he trusts Jim to notice it, too. Thus, as the book literally races toward its finish, we are rooting not only for Jim to win at the mile and get his grades; we are also rooting for him to wake up to what a fine young man he has become. This is a very warm kind of suspense. We like Jim, and we want him to like himself just as well.

The growth we see in Jim is, of course, one thing that is as true of college life today as it was in the 1930s. Freshman life has always offered kids the chance to lose themselves in extraneous enjoyments, or to immerse themselves in frantic academic or professional pursuit—or to balance fun and study and friendships, and grow up. *Iron Duke* gives perhaps the best pre-college lesson a high-school reader could get, and gives it lightly and realistically. Jim juggles his disappointments, fends off his confusion, and finds his way to several wonderful discoveries. He starts from scratch, without special gifts, and he makes mistakes, but at the end of the book he is doing interesting things, and doing them very well. He's not on a pinnacle, he's not a superstar—he's doing interesting things very well. That should be what every kid goes to college hoping to accomplish. For that matter, that's the hope he or she should take away from college, as the goal for a good life.

—Bruce Brooks

Iron Duke

1

The telephone downstairs woke him. On the faded wallpaper which was the first thing he saw every morning, a familiar patch of sunlight greeted his eyes. Terrifying to think that this was the last morning for eight months he would wake to see that patch on the wall. Now that he was really in for it, going east to college seemed like going to China.

"Jimmy."

"Yes, Mother."

"Mr. Foster. He wants to say good-bye. He's driving over to Cedar Rapids this morning and can't get down to the station."

He pulled on a bathrobe through which his elbows showed, and stumbled sleepily down-stairs. Through a daze he heard the booming voice of the minister who always made a speech when he talked, even over the telephone. "Great opportunity . . . we here in Waterloo are proud of you . . . grateful to your good father for the chance . . . the school will watch your career with . . . expect great things . . . advantages that others . . ." the sentences followed each other like balls down a bowling alley. He'd heard it all before; from Mr. Jamison, the vice-president of the Electric Light Company where he had worked all summer, from the editor of the *Courier*, from the secretary of the Y, in fact from everyone. It was only necessary to mumble a few words. "Yessir. Yessir. H'm, yessir, thanks very much, Mister Foster . . . yessir. Much obliged, sir . . . g'bye."

He hung up and went back upstairs, now thoroughly awakened. The moment the bathroom door was closed the telephone rang again. "No, you can't," said his mother. He could always tell when she was talking to one of his friends of the other sex by that unpleasant ring to her voice. What he called her girl-tone. "He isn't even up yet." She rang off more hurriedly than necessary and went back to the dining room. Her remarks to his father came to him from below. There was nothing original in them; both he and his father had listened many times to her views on modern girls. "Why, they don't even let him get his clothes on, those Parsons . . ." He turned the water full force in the bathtub so as to cut off the sound of her voice, because he knew exactly what was coming. How girls of her time would no more think of calling up a boy at his home and pestering him with invitations the way they did nowadays! And Father sitting at the breakfast table reading the *Courier* would agree not very enthusiastically. The idea occurred to him that maybe long ago Father had been called up and didn't care to admit it.

Back in his room, after the bath, he felt better. A trunk was open with clothes hanging over it, and three suitcases on the floor were open and piled with shirts, shoes, underclothes, and odd objects of wearing apparel. He turned on the radio. Last chance he'd have to hear the old station for eight months. This going away to college wasn't such a simple matter, especially when you were traveling half across a continent to school.

"Station KDVX, Waterloo, Iowa. You will now hear the City Songsters in their half hour program of fun and popular hits of the day. The first number, *My Heart Goes Out to You*. Take her away, George." And a volume of sound filled the room, while he opened drawers to find clean socks, and the shirt his mother had saved out specially for him.

"JIMMY. JIM—MY. SHUT OFF THAT RADIO. Your mother can't hear a thing, she's trying to talk on the telephone."

Holy smoke! Can't even listen to the radio on his last day home. His last few hours. From below his mother's voice came clearly up as he shut off George Bassett and his Swing Boys. "Well, the train leaves at ten-fifty, the Chief, you know." There was a touch of pride in her voice. When anyone in town spoke of the Chief, it meant a real journey, it meant you were going at least as far as Chicago if not further. For the Chief was the one limited train that touched at Waterloo. "Of course, I'm sure he'd love to have them. Of course he would. How thoughtful of you, Mrs. Davison. That's so kind. Oh, no, don't bother to come to the station, I'll have his father run over right now. No, don't you bother, Mr. Wellington is going right down town to do some last minute errands. Oh, yes, he has to pick up a pair of Jim's trousers at the cleaners. Goodbye, and thanks so much. . . ."

"MOTHER. That old hen isn't coming to the station, is she?" He leaned over the railing in the hall, his lanky body clothed in one sock and a pair of running trunks. "What does she want, anyway?"

"She says she's just baked a batch of brownies, and you always liked them, so she thought you might like to take a package along with you."

"But, gosh, Mother, won't you ever have any sense? How can a man going to college take a paper bag of cookies in his hand. How'd I look, huh? I sh'd think you'd have a better appreciation of the fact that I'm grown up and can't—"

"But, Jimmy, how could I refuse? I couldn't hurt her feelings. Besides, you can leave them in the train when you change at Chicago, or give them to the porter. What difference does it make? Now go get dressed. Your father will bring back your trousers."

When he came downstairs he found the *Courier* half opened on the table. It was opened to a picture of—of—it couldn't be! Yes, a picture of himself. "Local Boy Leaves Today for College in East. James H. Wellington's Son for Harvard."

"Hey, Mother. Did you see this? My photo's in the *Courier*."

His mother entered the room, bacon and eggs in her hand. "Yes, I know, we saw it. Come, eat your breakfast. Never mind the *Courier*. You can read that on the train. Oh, dear, there goes the doorbell again. What on earth can that be? It's Dorlons with your flannel trousers." He heard her voice talking with the cleaner's man at the door. "Yes, he's off in a short while now. Well, it's a long way, but he's anxious to go to his father's college."

Gosh, mothers didn't have any sense sometimes. Why did she have to discuss his personal business with the man from the cleaners? He was annoyed, but his annoyance didn't last long because his mind was on the column in the *Cou-*

rier. Naturally he'd been in the paper before, you couldn't get through High and play football without that. But this was a real story. "One of the most popular members of Waterloo's younger set . . . president of the senior class at Stimson High and end on last year's football eleven . . . son of James H. Wellington of the Ottumwa Valley Light and Power Co. . . ."

"Jimmy! Look, your eggs are all cold. Now do pay attention to your breakfast. Put the trousers in the trunk when you go upstairs. I must call Kiggins to make sure they come for it. There's Spot scratching at the door. Spot. Stop scratching." But Spot did not stop scratching. Like everyone else in the house he felt the unusual atmosphere existing. Something was about to happen. As she opened the front door, the big, clumsy Airedale charged in with leaps and bounds and rushed over to the master at the table, rubbing against his legs. "Hi, Spotty, old boy," said that young gentleman, his eyes half on his plate and half on the column before him. "Down, Spot. Down, Spotty. Yeah, sure gonna miss you, Spot, old boy. Take care of yourself, mind you don't go running off down Reynolds Avenue in that traffic. Will you, Spot, huh?" Thump-thump-thump went the dog's tail. Something special certainly was in the air. The front door slammed and his father came in with a big bundle.

"The woman's mad. There's enough brownies here to feed the whole freshman class at Harvard. Must think you're crazy. Take a couple in your overcoat pocket, Jim, and we'll shove the rest under the sofa until you're gone. Think this family will be living on brownies until Christmas. Just send the old girl a line and thank her, won't you?"

"Uhuh. Yes, Father."

"There they are! Those trousers. They said they'd sent them up and I swore they hadn't. Take 'em up and pack 'em before you forget it."

Jim ran upstairs to finish packing, Spot galumping along at his heels. By this time Spot was sure something really was behind these preparations. It wasn't just a fishing trip up the river. No, this was business. Tail between his legs he followed his master, now into the big front room, now back into his own bedroom, downstairs, then back up again. Once there he climbed on the bed, and when this usually forbidden move was greeted by a caress and not a scolding, he was acutely aware of something unpleasant going to happen soon.

Jim took the gray flannel trousers and tried to make them fit over the clothes hung on hangers in the trunk. That made it impossible to shut the bulging thing. In fact, it couldn't even be shut as it was, so he had to repack it completely, taking out one whole suit, folding it and placing it in a suitcase. Then at last the trunk closed. One after another he opened and examined carefully each drawer in his dresser to make sure he hadn't left anything. Downstairs the telephone was ringing eternally. At that moment a car stopped outside. His father answered the telephone, while in a minute his mother called from the front hall.

"Jim! Is your trunk ready? Here's Kiggins' man."

"All ready, Mother." The man came up and, grabbing the trunk, bumped off downstairs. Jim shoved the pictures of his father and mother into the last remaining suitcase that was open, and pushed it into the hall. A final glance about the room. This going so far away to college had its bad points. Now that he was actually at the moment of leaving, he hated to go. Yet he had been looking forward to it all summer. All year. In fact all through school. And now it was here he didn't want to go. He heard his father on the stairs, and putting those thoughts from his mind, handed him one of the suitcases while he followed with two others and Spot brought up the end. All his baggage was now in the lower hall. The clock inside the front room chimed ten. It gave him that unpleasant feeling once more to realize that he wouldn't hear the clock for months and months. Exciting, this going to college. Yes, and unpleasant, too.

His mother came from the kitchen. "Did you pack your brownies?" He looked at his father and his father looked at him, but she went on. "Have you got your ticket? Sure? And your money?" He felt in his inside pocket for the long envelope with the green ticket to Boston. There it was. His money was in his purse in his left back pocket. He took it out and carefully counted it. "Jim, I do wish—I think that's awfully dangerous, carrying all that money in your back pocket."

"Now, Helen, let the boy carry it anywhere he wants to. He's old enough—"

"I know, but suppose he loses fifty dollars? What then? Have you got everything now? That admission certificate; the thing they sent you from Cambridge?"

"Gosh! Have I? Didn't you put that in the folder in the trunk? You didn't? Neither did I. Where is it?" Everyone dissolved in different directions. He ran upstairs, pulling out the papers on his own study desk. His mother looked through her desk in the front room, while Father was going over a pile of stuff on the living room table. Spot, uncertain whom to follow, and afraid of missing something important, stood hesitating at the bottom of the stairs. Then he clambered up after the boss.

Of course his mother was the one to find the precious document. She was always the one to find things. There was a reason why she should be the one to find this. A few days before she had extracted it from the folder in his trunk to show a neighbor. For that piece of paper, with the seal of the college and the plain statement that James H. Wellington, Jr., of Waterloo, Iowa, had been admitted to the freshman class with honors in history, gave her a surge of pride. Down the stairs two at a time came Jim, behind him Spot, slipping and sliding to the bottom. He grabbed the paper and, opening a suitcase, shoved it inside.

"Now. All set. My tennis bat. Where is it? You take that, Dad. Good-bye, Spot, old boy. 'Bye, old boy. Stick up that tail, hey, kid." He took his mother in his arms. "Good-bye, Mother. Be sure and wear your rubbers. Remember I won't be here to look after you." She laughed, but it was a hollow laugh. Down the steps into the car. The family had agreed it was better for her not to come to the station. They didn't, as a family, enjoy public farewells. Inside he hurled the last two suitcases. His head followed them, when suddenly it emerged.

"My skis." In the hurry everyone had forgotten the skis. He dashed up the steps, Spot barking with delight. Maybe the boss wasn't leaving after all. The skis were standing on end in the garage, carefully wrapped in cloth and ready to be tied on the car. He ran out with them, leaned them on the front wheel's mudguard, took one deft twist with the rope round the door handle, and, shoving the poles in, jumped in beside his father on the front seat. Above stood his mother on the front step. Spot's disconsolate face showed for just a second. "Let's go, Dad."

The run to the station took hardly five minutes. Neither said much. As they drew up before the entrance, his father noticed a crowd about the door. "Hullo, look at that turnout. What do you suppose—"

As soon as the car stopped, they were surrounded. Jim and Eddie and Marshall Smith and Bill and Henry and all his friends; in fact about the whole school was there. Also the band. "Well, of all the darn fool things," he muttered to himself. This was pretty bad. If only he'd thought, Dad could have driven him over to take the train at Cedar Rapids.

Someone unloosened the skis. Someone else reached in and handed out his suitcases that were grabbed by willing hands. Someone took his tennis racket from him, and someone hustled him through the station out to the platform. Worse to come. Because there was Mr. Philips, the high school principal, with Bud Smith, captain of last year's eleven, who was going to matriculate at State that next week. And Mr. Donaldson, the president of the Chamber of Commerce and a friend of Dad's, and Nick Devine, reporter from the *Courier*.

They formed a semicircle around him. Behind the circle clustered a growing group of loafers, travelers, several trainmen, a couple of dozen kids attracted by the band, and the one station porter in his red cap which he donned every day just before the Chief was due in town. As the band which had escorted him through the station ended its number, Mr. Philips stepped forward. The crowd pushed closer, making the semicircle smaller. "Remarkable record these last four years . . . first boy to enter an eastern college with honors since . . . no graduate of Stimson High ever before . . . it therefore gives me much pleasure to present you this watch which takes with it all our best and heartiest good wishes." And he handed a small package to Jim who fumblingly began to open it.

Before he could even tear or undo the string, before he had time to mumble more than a few words of thanks, there was a shriek and a roar and the platform trembled as the Chief thundered into the train shed, punctual to the minute. It covered the band, the principal, his father and the onlookers with a thick cloud of dust, smoke, and cinders. With a sigh from the engine up front the express came slowly to a stop.

Just what was going on the passengers in the observation car did not know. But evidently something of importance was taking place on the platform below their eyes. Stirred from the lethargy of a long morning aboard a train, they crowded to the windows and watched the proceedings with interest as the band burst into music and a tall youth in a polo coat was surrounded by a crowd of handshakers and backslappers. The grinning faces from the window just above added to Jim's embarrassment. With relief he heard the conductor call, "All aboard."

Someone handed up his bags. A porter shoved his skis aboard. "G'bye, Dad. G'bye, Bill. So long, Tommy. G'bye, Jim." He took his tennis racket in one hand and, waving thanks with the package in the other, entered the car. The occupants stuck their faces out into the aisle, curious to see the celebrity who was about to join them. His seat was just above the awful crowd on the platform, the noisy band, the eager voices shouting to make themselves heard through the two thick windows of the Pullman. He realized his face was red, his forehead sweating. Luckily the Chief only hesitated at Waterloo. There was a jerk. The train was moving. Slowly she started pulling away from the crowd on the platform.

The boys and girls below walked alongside the train as it moved. Faces he'd grown up with, faces of those he'd gone with to school, sat beside in class, played with on the field, swam with in the lake in summer. The music became fainter and the knot of older folks in the rear became dimmer, when his eye caught a figure hurrying across the tracks from the station. It couldn't be! It was. His mother, and under her arm were the flannel trousers and in her hand was the bag of brownies.

He couldn't believe it. But there she was, holding them up for him to see. Sometimes mothers just had no sense at all. He pretended he didn't see her. But every face at the car windows saw her, and knew what she wanted. Gently the car gathered speed. She handed the trousers and the bundle to some boy who started to run after the last car. There was a commotion aboard. Would they make the train or not? Only Jim was indifferent. In a minute the car was out from under the roof into sunlight, going through the east end of town. The door at the rear opened, and the porter of the observation car appeared with the trousers rolled up under his arm, and that enormous bag of brownies in his other hand.

A regular chorus of approval greeted him as he made his way down the aisle. To Jim's chagrin he was spotted immediately.

"Yessah, yessah, yo' mother's right smart woman, she sure is. . . ."

2

Jim climbed the three flights of stairs to his room tucked away under the roof of Lionel. Beneath the door stuck the edge of a card. Gosh, what now!

"You will report for a voice test on Tuesday, October third at ten-thirty at Memorial Hall."

Voice test. Say, what did they think he came to college for? To be a movie actor? Already in one short week he had been through so many tests, conferences, and meetings, that he was dizzy. First, registration. That took two whole days. Then after this complicated process came a conference with his adviser, an oldish-young man in a dormitory by the river. This gentleman named Mason was friendly and agreeable and told him to drop in whenever he needed help. When trouble came later, he found it impossible to see his adviser unless the secretary made an appointment ten days in advance. A physical examination took the best part of an afternoon. A conducted tour of the Library lasted longer. A meeting of the class was held in the New Lecture Hall—typical, he thought, that here at Cambridge they called a place fifty years old, new—to explain the athletic and extracurricular activities of the University. It was addressed among others by the football captain who asked each man to shake hands with the fellow next and introduce himself. Everyone did, with some reluctance, and then forgot to whom he had spoken. Finally there was a meeting of the entire freshman class, addressed by the president, a thinnish man with a hard, nasal New England accent, and a sense of humor, who said among other things:

"Take a good look at me, for the chances are

you won't see me again until you graduate." A remark that seemed to typify the impersonal attitude of the place. You came and did what you liked. No one bothered much where you went, what courses you took, how you spent your time. Now at Stimson High, you saw the principal whenever you liked—too often, in fact.

Cambridge was terrifying. A thousand and twenty freshmen! Why, that was almost twice as many as in the whole of Grinnell College back home, and Grinnell was considered a pretty fair-sized place. Dozens of strange buildings whose names it was impossible to remember. Three different libraries; Widener, one in the Union reserved for freshmen, and a history library somewhere he had yet to discover. Enormous classes. In History 1 there were eight hundred. That was about the total number at Stimson.

The size of the class made it hard to know anyone. At the Union where they all ate, you grabbed a seat, gobbled your food, and went out without a word to the man next to you. If, indeed, there was a man next to you. He found that when he sat down at an empty table, men came in and crowded at the other end as though he had leprosy. This meant he had to eat frequently alone, a thing he had never done and dreaded. One noon in desperation he made some innocuous remark to the waitress and before long was involved in a harmless and meaningless conversation. Suddenly one of the head waitresses loomed up before him wearing a highly significant smirk. Conversation ended. His meal was concluded in silence and he never spoke again to the waitress except to order a meal.

Already he had discovered one thing. Coming from a middle western high school certainly made things difficult. The groups from the big preparatory schools kept together in shoals. Exeter, Choate, Groton, and the large eastern academies sent delegations who roomed with each other in the same entries in the same buildings, hung together after class, trooped into the Union for meals in a unit. In fact, they were small units in the life of the class. These men all had friends and wanted no more. Back in Waterloo he spoke to everyone in school whether he actually knew them or not; in this way he'd made lots of interesting friends. Such a procedure didn't work at Cambridge. There was the man who sat two seats from him in History, whom he met every morning going to breakfast. When that man failed to reply to his greeting one morning, he thought probably he hadn't noticed. But when this happened two successive days, the snub direct hurt. That sort of thing was a new experience. He was unaccustomed to it, it made something inside sore and raw all the rest of the week. Useless to tell himself it didn't matter, that he was super-sensitive, for the episode remained vivid, unforgettable. It was all very confusing and accentuated his loneliness.

Work, too, was difficult. No end to the work. Every instructor and professor seemed to think his course was the only one in college and threw out lists of books to read and assignments without end. As an honor man at Stimson High, Jim had felt little apprehension over the actual work, but shocks came fast and early. Everyone to get an A.B. degree had to pass a reading examination in either French or German. You could take this examination any time, or as often as you liked, and some tried at the start of their freshmen year. Naturally, he told himself, if it was as stiff as they said, he mightn't pass. Then again he might. He was second from the top in French at Stimson, and he imagined Mr. Boyce, the teacher, was pretty good. He certainly talked French like anything. That examination, however, was a shock. It opened his eyes to standards he hadn't dreamed about. In the reading passage they were given were words he'd never seen, sentences he couldn't understand, idioms that meant nothing. Each student was allowed five mistakes in the two pages of translation. Going dolefully on afterward to dinner, he was aware he made at least fifty.

Back later to his room. The first few days it had seemed impossible to live there. The bed was hard with a thin mattress. Worse still, it was under a window that gave out onto the Square where traffic roared past night and day, at night even more insistently than by day. Nearby was the subway to Boston which shook the building every few minutes. Several weeks passed before he was able to sleep well. He therefore climbed the stairs that evening without much enthusiasm, remembering his own comfortable bed at home he'd been so anxious to leave. That made him remember he hadn't written home for a week. When there wasn't much good news, you couldn't write. But he must. Either Father or Mother wrote him every day, and he depended on their letters.

A door was half open on the floor just below his. Inside a figure with its feet on the desk and a cigarette in its mouth looked out. Jim started to say hullo, hesitated, mumbled something in confusion, and was passing upstairs when the man within called out.

"Hi, freshman."

He turned and looked back. "Hullo."

"Come in . . . have a chair. You live up above, don't you?" The cigarette remained in the corner of his mouth and he stayed seated, but at least his tone was friendly. He was the second person in two weeks who had spoken voluntarily. He seemed a bit too old for a freshman. Evidently Irish. A ruddy face. Strong, stocky figure. Wide shoulders. Nice grin.

"Yeah. 32."

"Oh. You in 32, are you? Right above me. Where you come from?"

"Waterloo, Iowa. Name's Wellington. James H. Wellington." Now that remark at home always brought a sudden response. "Oh, you Jim Wellington's boy, are you?" He hadn't heard it since leaving, but there was the same quick response in the man's face.

"Wellington. Wellington! Wellington-Waterloo. That's good, that is. The Iron Duke. Now whaddye think of that?"

A reflection that possibly the scholastic standards of Stimson High were not as severe as he had imagined, a feeling engendered by the disastrous examination of the afternoon, was strengthened by this remark. Hastily he searched through the files of his memory. Wellington-Waterloo. Why, sure. Of course. Wellington-Waterloo. He'd never thought of it.

"Yeah. I never happened to think of that. Iron Duke. Say, that's funny, isn't it. Folks always called me Jim at home. I guess I'm not much of an Iron Duke. This place has me dizzy already."

"Well, we'll have to call you Duke. Just plain Duke. Take it easy, kid. Don't let 'em get you down at first. They love to, you know. It's hard finding your feet when you get shoved into a big place like this. Where'd you say you were from?"

"Waterloo, Iowa."

"Yeah, I know—but high school?"

"Uhuh. Stimson High. Best school in the state."

"Sure? You wouldn't fool me, would you?" What'd he mean by that?

Just then a figure appeared in the half-opened doorway, and the owner of the room greeted him. "Hullo, handsome, come in and take a load off those good-looking feet of yours."

He was tall, blond, elegantly dressed and perfectly assured. These contained individuals were a new type to Jim, and they were to be found all over the place, disturbed by nothing and no one. "Thanks," he said. "They are rather good-looking, aren't they? Is this a conference?"

"Not at all," said the man with the cigarette. He waved his hand to a chair and remarked as an introduction,

"My name you saw on the door—McGuire. They call me Mickey. I observed you looking at it before you knocked." In Waterloo this would border on rudeness, but the newcomer didn't seem to notice. "This gentleman here is the Iron Duke. We all call him Duke, for short." Who was the "all," Jim wondered. "He comes from a town named Waterloo in the state of Iowa. Out where the tall corn grows. Ever hear of it? I thought not. Well, his name is Wellington. I trust you get the connection."

"Without a map," replied the stranger, favoring Jim with a nod. "I am the bearer of the distinguished name of Smith. Not that it matters." This was a disappointment. To one whose manners like his clothes and his accent bordered on the aristocratic, Smith unquestionably was a letdown. He should bear a name to match.

"If I appear to intrude, throw me out. I'm merely asking a slight favor. Collection to take the freshman band to the Yale game. Do you . . ."

Jim did a hasty calculation. Already his expenses had been twice what he had allowed. Books. Subscription to the *Crimson* and *Lampoon*. Laboratory fees. It was very confusing. This man with his lofty manners would be a tough bird to refuse. Especially since it was to support the team. One ought to support the team, of course. To his surprise and relief, the owner of the room spoke.

"Sorry. No customers here. We're all anti-football here. Think it's a racket."

More astonishing still, the elegant youth agreed heartily. "Quite so. It is, isn't it? But after all, what isn't a racket these days? And it does amuse the populace, you'll admit."

As an answer the Irishman rose and went over to the window. Jim saw how sturdily he was built, good football material whether he liked the game or not. The window rose with a bang, and through the moist October evening came shouts from below.

"RHINEHART . . . Rhinehart . . . oh . . . Rhinehart . . ."

"Say. That looks like trouble." The noise and

the shouts increased. They were confused with an occasional "Rhinehart." The two others moved to the window. Below in the Yard, a mass of freshmen were festering round a building at the end. There seemed to be no direction or leader, but certainly something was about to happen. From every side and from the entry to every dormitory, men could be seen running to join the mob. The Irishman banged down the window. There was elation in his tone.

"Gents, that sure looks like trouble. Let's go."

Three steps at a time they ran down to the ground.

3

Reaching the ground, they found the mob at the end of the Yard moving slowly toward the Gate to the Square. It was growing larger every minute as individuals rushed from each entry to join. "Keep together. Stay with me, you fellows," shouted McGuire to his companions, linking his arms in theirs when they fell into line at the rear of the procession. Jim had never seen a huge crowd like this. For the first time since arriving at Cambridge he became part of a great body and not an isolated unit in a friend-less organization. It was exciting but terrifying, because he could feel the force of those marching hundreds. A policeman standing just beyond the gate felt it, also. He stood hesitating, not sure whether to interfere, when an eddy of men swept him away. No one actually hit him, but the move-ment of a dozen bodies swinging in unison pushed him to one side and he spun round and almost fell. They moved into the open spaces of the Square between the Yard and the church across the way, completely stopping the cross traffic of cars and trucks.

Slowly, inch by inch, its bell clanging fu-riously, a trolley attempted to pass through. It was working along at a walk, the passengers within standing up and peering through the win-dows much as the alarmed passengers of a car-avan might gaze down on an aroused tribe in the African bush. Suddenly McGuire's powerful voice rose above the roar.

"Hey, there. Grab that rope. The trolley rope." No one heard. Or if they heard no one paid any attention. With a gesture of impatience he left his companions and shoved forward, his pow-erful shoulders making a path to the back of the car. Then with a jump he climbed up the rear end, reached the trolley wire, and pulled it from the overhead suspension. Instantly the car went black and it stopped short.

The door opened. In it stood the motorman, his handle in his upraised hand, shouting at the swirling crowd below. A cheer taunted him. For a minute he answered back, then thinking better of it he reached over and closed the door with a bang. The jeers from the crowd increased. Meanwhile, pressure from the back of the throng began to move the car so that it swayed gently from side to side. Here was an idea. Ten, twenty, fifty men began to push against it. The car rocked, slowly at first, then violently. Inside the frightened passengers clung to straps and hung to their seats, expecting the worst at any moment. Then above the noise and shouts came the clang-clang-clang of a patrol wagon. Someone had turned in a riot call.

"That's Apted, did that," shouted a boy next to Jim. He had no idea who Apted was. Already twenty Cambridge coppers in a police car charged through Church Street, and reaching the scene of trouble, disembarked and began whacking their way with sticks to the beleaguered trolley.

None too soon, either. It was teetering more and more as the pressure increased.

"Cops! Cops!" was the warning cry. The mob melted to one side while the police clubbed their path to the car. The passengers descended like prisoners from a besieged castle. From a hundred throats rose the cry. "Apted. Apted. Get Apted."

"Who's that? Who're they after?" asked the Duke, breathless and excited. He managed to rejoin his friends. McGuire was now hatless with a rent up the side of his coat.

"Colonel Apted. He's the Superintendent of Buildings. They're going to kidnap him." It was a good idea but that worthy had evidently heard their cries, for his office was locked and empty. For a while the mob milled round. Suddenly McGuire had an idea.

"The clapper! Let's get the clapper." This produced a reaction of delight and with a shout the big crowd moved across the Yard to the Chapel. The Chapel bell woke every freshman and everyone else in the vicinity each morning at seven with its boisterous clanging. The idea was therefore popular. McGuire lost his companions in the rush over to the Chapel and they waited below while with several others he climbed the tower, forced the door, and finally reappeared below with the clapper from the bell.

Again shouts. "To Radcliffe." "On to Radcliffe." "Take it up to Radcliffe." They went across the Yard, the crowd increasing, and as they poured out the gate a little man with glasses stood with pencil and paper vainly trying to get their names while they passed. "It's the head proctor . . . McDonald . . . fat chance he has in this crowd. . . ." The proctor was shoved to one side, the paper snatched from his hand, and once again they were outside in the Square.

By this time, they were at least a thousand. McGuire had taken command, and, lugging the clapper, he moved across the Square to a telegraph pole and started to climb. The crowd objected.

"To Radcliffe. Let's take it up to Radcliffe." But he paid no attention except to gesticulate for aid. Someone gave him a shove and by reaching he managed to grab the first hook and pull himself up. There was a cheer as he leaned down and took the clapper. Slowly he mounted the pole, and carefully placed the clapper over one of the covered wires on the cross-arm. There was a sparkle and the adjacent street lamps went out.

This was too much for the brigade of police who had been viewing the proceedings from a safe distance across the Square. They charged over into the mob which became a melee of flashing sticks, hands, arms, coats and hats. Outnumbered and outfought, they soon retreated, bearing two battered-looking freshmen as hostages. From the rear where he stood Jim could hear the voice of his Irish friend.

"Come on, freshmen, come on, get 'em from those mugs." Action was exactly what the crowd most desired and as a unit they descended on the little knot of blue. The scrap was short and sharp. In a minute the two prisoners were free. To be sure, a price had been paid. Cracked heads, bruised faces, and black eyes told the story. But the freshmen were safe, and one or two even wore a blue policeman's cap or waved a nightstick to taunt the forces of the law.

Then the sharp shrill whistle of authority sounded in the cool night air, bringing news of approaching reinforcements. It also drew boos from the crowd when a minute later a fire truck surged into the Square and firemen, jumping out, attached an enormous hose to a hydrant. Behind them another police car loaded with men roared into action. The Square was a battlefield. Hats, caps, and torn garments were scattered about, and by this time traffic was so tied up that most of the streets leading into Massachusetts Avenue were a mass of honking cars unable to move.

"Now, boys. Before they get it hitched up." Once more the undergraduates rushed across the Square, charging the firemen in an effort to reach them before the hose was working. It was a close race. The freshmen won, but not before the final twist of the big wrench had been given and the water spurted, knocking down half a dozen in its path. Then the hose was pulled from the hands of the firemen, and sizzled harmlessly on the ground.

However, reinforcements for the law were arriving from every quarter. The Cambridgeport station, called by telephone, had responded with two truckloads of men who came up Cambridge Street and took the mob in the rear. Aided by gas bombs which caused everyone in the vicinity to dissolve in tears, they cut a path through the mob to the beleaguered firemen, using their clubs to such effect that opponents went down right and left. Separated from his friends, Jim was pushing or being pushed toward the front and knew nothing of the arrival of the police behind. Suddenly the pressure became greater. He felt himself shoved violently to one side, there were shouts and cries and then something struck him a savage blow over the head that made him so dizzy he sank to the ground and would have been tramped upon had not friendly arms pulled him up and away.

Instantly the mob melted. From every street came the clanging of bells that told of more police joining the fray. The effect of the tear gas was to clear wide spaces. Cops were now everywhere and in complete command. Jim staggered to the curb, his only thought to reach his room and lie down, for he was getting dizzier each minute. At last he reached the gate, swaying as he walked. By the entrance stood the little bespectacled proctor, considerably mussed but still able to take names of the onrushing crowd. Then Jim realized he was fainting. He was going to fall. He did fall—when someone caught him.

Of course, he didn't know that McGuire had been following him and trying to reach him through the mob, now cowed and panic-stricken like all mobs. As he came to, he was leaning against the iron fence, the Irishman standing over him.

"Hey, Smith. Hey there, you, blondy. C'm here!" He felt himself dragged and hustled through the gate with a mass of others at such a pace the proctor hardly got more than a look at them. Then to the dormitory. Up the stairs. In a minute he was stretched on the couch in McGuire's bedroom, his head being bathed and the blood wiped from his clotted hair.

"Here. Look out. Lemme see. Naw. That's nothing. Nothing at all. I've had worse bumps than that in a football game and kept on playing. So've you. Sure. Just stay there and rest, Duke. Hey, kid!" The Irishman grinned down at him. "Here, you . . ." this to Smith. "Take this basin and fill it with water. Keep his head damp, see. What's your name, d'you say?"

"Smith. J. Faugeres Smith, if that means anything to you."

Somehow the Duke was relieved. Even with collar torn and necktie awry, this youth had an air and manner that did not sit well with the name of Smith. Faugeres! There was a title becoming him. Jim's head ached terribly, throbbed rather, but through the throbbing he approved of that name. It gave the blond youth the necessary distinction. But it didn't seem to go down so well with McGuire. "Faugeres! Well, we'll call you Fog around here. Just plain Fog, see? Now, Fog, snap to it. This is a bad spot right now. In ten minutes the place will be stinking with proctors. Sure it will. If we aren't smart we'll be on probation with half this class. I'll give a quick wash and change my rig. Keep the bedroom door open . . . no, half open, like that, so it hides the bed, that's all."

"But then the proctors can come right in—"

"Sure they can. But listen, stupid, they're much more likely to come in if the door's shut. If it's ajar like this, see, they may not bother to look inside carefully. Keep quiet when they come and don't move. Now do what I tell you." And he began washing his face and hands and changing his clothes. In four or five minutes he was in his swivel chair in the other room, hardly too soon, either. There was a determined tramp on the stairs, and an unpleasantly authoritative voice spoke as someone knocked on the door.

"Yep. Come in." The door opened and in walked the disheveled proctor and a policeman much the worse for wear. McGuire stared at them as if he had never seen such sights, as if he had not himself looked like them ten minutes before. They saw a ruddy-faced Irish boy sitting with a book in his lap and his feet on a desk which also supported an open textbook. A half-smoked cigarette was in his mouth and he had the general appearance of having been in that position all evening.

"Your name, please," said the proctor. There were scratches on his face, one trouser leg was ripped and torn, and his glasses were broken. But his condition was nothing compared to the policeman who could hardly walk. He leaned heavily against the edge of the door as the proctor cross-examined McGuire.

"McGuire, Joseph P."

"Freshman?"

"Yes, sir. What's the trouble?"

"There's been a riot in the Square. Most of the freshman class were participating. Were you out this evening?"

McGuire's bland innocence was beautiful to behold from the darkened bedroom.

"With the amount of work I've got to do to get ready for a history section tomorrow, how could I go out?"

The proctor took a different tack. "Whose section are you in?"

"Mr. Longstreeth's." The proctor happened to know that Longstreeth had a section meeting in history the next day. And after all, there were the book, the notes, and the cigarette. And he certainly didn't have the disheveled appearance of his visitors.

"Officer! Do you recognize this man?"

The cop who was minus his cap and plus a nasty bruise on his forehead, looked intently. McGuire returned the stare coolly.

"I do . . . and then again I don't, sir. So many of 'em, you might say . . . and all at once they came, like. He might be him that climbed up with the clapper. No. That one had on a gray suit."

"You wouldn't swear?"

"Swear? I couldn't, sir. It might be him. Then again . . ."

This wasn't getting anywhere. The proctor had thirty more rooms in the building to cover in the next half hour. He couldn't waste time on uncertainties. There were too many whose torn bodies would betray their participation.

"Your roommate. Is he in there?" Indicating

the bedroom. Inside, the two on the bed hardly dared listen to the answer. But it came, clear and disarming.

"No, sir, I room alone."

"Of course. These are single rooms up here. I forgot. Who rooms above?"

"A man from the west named Wellington."

"Has he a roommate?"

"No, sir, he rooms alone, too."

"All right. Mr. McGuire, no one is to leave the building tonight. Understand?"

"Yes, sir, I understand." The door closed on the proctor and the officer. They tramped downstairs and could be heard banging on the door of the room of the unfortunates just below.

4

When he reported for freshman football at the locker building that sunny September afternoon, the lost feeling he had felt since his arrival was accentuated. Like everything else, the business of football here was on a tremendous scale. You were a private in an army, not a member of a football team. The freshmen rolled up in dozens; huge backs, husky linemen, giant ends and quarters. There were, it seemed, more managers and assistant managers than players at Stimson High. They were needed, too. The first day was one of passing in review before long tables at which one's entire history—and especially one's athletic history—was noted on big cards. Name. Age. Weight. Position. Experience. School. Years. First string or substitute. Father ever play. Endlessly the questions were hurled at him. He listened to boys about him being cross-examined, heard names of schools he never knew existed. Everyone seemed to come from a different place. Solemnly drawing his equipment and finding a locker took most of the afternoon. He walked alone up to the Yard, overcome by a forlorn homesickness. To be sure, he had realized that standards of football at Cambridge would be high. That making a place on the freshman eleven would be difficult, no matter what the boys at home said. He wished ruefully that Jim and Ed and Marshall Smith who played with him could see that mob. There was a fight ahead, no matter what they might think. As he crossed the Anderson Bridge on the way back to his room, he overheard two boys, also candidates, discussing the situation.

"They said two hundred and eight. Think of it, two hundred men for eleven places."

That didn't help. He'd be lucky if he managed to stay on the squad, let alone make the team.

Practice the next afternoon was not more reassuring. These boys were big, rangy, and their knowledge of football fundamentals was much beyond his own. The fact that he knew not a soul on the squad didn't help. Only one person spoke to him that first week. McGuire took the trouble to trot over across the field where Jim stood waiting a chance at the tackling dummy.

"Hi, boy. How'aryuh, Duke?" The name was unfamiliar, but the voice cheered him. He stammered—

"I—I don't know, exactly. This place . . . it's so big . . . so sort of . . ."

"Yeah, I know. It's tough when you aren't used to things. You'll get onto it, Duke, in a few days. Don't let 'em ride you. They try to ride everyone. Keep your chin up, kid." He patted him on the back and trotted back across the field, a compact, workmanlike figure in his red jersey and new trousers. He seemed a real player, equal to any situation.

The next afternoon there were scrimmages for four elevens, at none of which did Jim take part. To his astonishment, he found that scrimmages weren't just scrimmages as they were back home; they were modified, dummy, mock, skeleton, hard or something else. Every day there was a different kind of a scrimmage, and although the squad had been cut in half, he still watched with about a hundred others from the stands. The freshman coach, a tall man in baseball pants and a sweatshirt with a baseball cap pulled down over his eyes, stood overseeing the two first teams closely. He had a curt, unfriendly manner, in contrast to the gentle, familiar ways of Mr. Barnes back home who was football coach and mathematics teacher and thus able to call everyone on the squad by his first name.

Late the fifth day, the Duke had still to get into action. There were others. Beside him in the bleachers, listening to the coach bark commands, sat almost fifty players. On the field the two teams were in a deadlock when the horn sounded and the coach turned toward them. For a minute he looked the group over, and then shouted in a surly voice.

"McGuire." No one responded. "McGuire!" From somewhere in back there was a stir. Usually the mere sound of the coach's voice calling a name acted as an electric shock. The boy would jump up, nervously throw off his coat, and dash onto the field. But this time things moved slowly. Gradually a figure worked its way into the front ranks and stepped down. Everyone turned to watch his progress.

"McGuire, they tell me you think you can play football. Go out there and let's see what you can do."

"Who is he?" whispered the Duke to the man next.

"McGuire. Mickey McGuire. Last year's Andover captain. He won the Exeter game alone." There was electricity in the air.

On the field the two teams stood waiting, the tenseness of the situation communicating itself to them. The coach, hands on his hips, watched as the sturdy composed figure of Jim's friend stood before the crowd and started slowly to peel off an Andover sweater turned inside out. He was the acme of self-possession. A murmur ran through the stand. Everyone could feel the clash of personalities, the dominating coach, the assured youngster in uniform. He tossed the sweater casually over to one side, hitched up his belt, and then looking the coach full in the face, passed him at a dog trot, pulling on his headgear as he went to take his place on the field.

"Who? Who'd you say?" Jim wanted to be sure.

"McGuire. Captain at Andover last year. He's a tough bird. The coach is trying to show him up."

Why should a coach want to show a man up? Why shouldn't a coach welcome a good player on his team? These and a dozen other questions came to him. But the moment was important. He watched McGuire take his place as quarterback on one team. He'll probably try a forward, thought Jim. No, he was carrying the ball himself. A gasp at his audaciousness swept over the stands. It was almost as if the player had turned and thumbed his nose at the coach. The crowd approved, and the approval became audible when the ball carrier, pushing behind his interference, found a hole and swept down the field.

His reactions were fast. One minute he was running well behind the two backs, then suddenly with a burst he was between them and away. He edged past one secondary defenseman, sucked in another, and drew away until only one player, nervously waiting far down the gridiron, stood between him and the goal. But instead of rushing on for a possible spectacular touchdown, he stopped, put the ball on the ground as if to say: there, that's what I can do! Then he returned to the mass of players in the rear. All eyes were now on the coach, red of face and angry.

"Waddya think this is, McGuire? This isn't any school outfit. We run 'em out here."

The sturdy figure in red stopped short. He looked over at the glaring coach, megaphone in hand. Would he speak? He hesitated, then went back to the scrimmage line in midfield again and called his team into a huddle.

To get away with it once was one thing. Surely he'd hardly dare try it again. The crowd edged forward in their seats as the huddle disinte-grated, the line jumped back into position, and the ball was passed. Surely not this time. Yes, there he was, calmly waiting with the ball in his hands. Then suddenly seeing a hole between guard and tackle, he was off. Past the line, straight-arming the secondary, he dodged one tackler with a beautiful swerve to the side, and once more was in open sea with that solitary defenseman anxiously treading ground as he ap-proached. Then again he stopped and placed the ball on the ground. The crowd in the bleachers gasped.

Up went the megaphone of the coach.

"McGuire! I told you to run 'em out. I'm boss here. Players on this field do what they're told. Understand?"

The boy stopped short. The hostility of the two men was evident. Each one had the temperament and the personality to annoy the other. The red deepened under the baseball cap as the coach turned to the bleachers. In a quiet tone he said, "Johnson, at right tackle. Peabody, plug up that hole at left guard. Saltonstall, go in at left end. Morehead, number two back. James, center. Get out there, you men, and stop that fellow dead, understand?"

A hurried, quick flinging of coats to the ground. Confusion in the stands as sweaters were tossed aside and headguards pulled on, and then five substitutes ran out into the lineup opposing McGuire. He stood erect for a minute behind his line, surveying the scene, contemptuous of the newcomers and expressing that contempt in a voice which didn't quite carry over to the stand. His words caused a nervous, uneasy shifting of feet among the newcomers. Then he called his team back into a huddle.

Would he tempt Fate a third time? Would he dare take the ball once more? Yes, he had it.

For a few seconds he was lost in a swarm of onrushing tacklers who seemed to surround him, then by magic he appeared in their backfield, his shifty figure dodging one man, holding the ball out to an opponent and pulling it away again, deftly sidestepping someone who had tried to knock him off his stride by hurling through the air, and finally moving competently down the field.

"Get him, get that man," shouted the coach, forgetting himself in the excitement of the moment.

But they couldn't get him. They surrounded him, they touched him, they jarred him and made him spin round, they dived for him and pawed at him and tackled him and slid off. They stopped his progress to the left, but he slipped through a hole to the right. Until he was free. Running gracefully and with perfect control and coordination, he raced past the secondary and swept toward the goal and the solitary defenseman. Now it was up to this last man. Unless McGuire placed the ball down. But this time he kept on. The crouching figure stood tense and nervous, on his toes and ready to jump to either side. Instead the carrier neither paused nor changed pace. He charged into, through, and over the waiting tackler. There was a waving of arms in the air, a clash of bodies, a figure rolling on the ground, and McGuire galloped across the goal line.

The face of the coach was purple. Around Jim was a chorus of involuntary exclamations. They didn't dare cheer, but they were unable to suppress their admiration as the stocky figure trotted back with the ball under his arm. Once was lucky, twice, maybe, but three times, no, that was football. They watched him come directly toward them, for he didn't go back to the scrimmage line in midfield. Instead, he came up to the coach. The stand was silent. Even the players on the field stood watching as he panted toward the figure with the megaphone beside the bleachers.

"I . . . ran it out . . . see?" He was breathing hard. Now he came nearer. "I ran it out . . . see . . . now then . . . take this . . ." A gasp came from the stand. He threw the football which hit the coach squarely on the chest, bounced off and bobbled at his feet.

The tall man stood motionless. His voice was dry and queer. "McGuire, turn in your uniform."

The boy as he threw the ball, ran past without pausing. He reached down, picked up his sweater, flung it over his shoulder and called back,

"That's just what . . . what I was going to do, Mister Coach . . ." and his figure disappeared behind the scenes.

5

During dinner that evening the Duke saw Fog wandering alone among the tables looking for him. That sight gave him the first warm feeling he had had since reaching Cambridge. Someone at last was anxious to see him. The fact was that anyone on the squad was sought, for rumors of the incident seemed to have gone the rounds. Men who never played football, men who never went to games, men who cared nothing about the sport were talking of the way that last year's

Andover captain had talked back to the freshman coach. The rumors grew until assault was the least that had been committed, because only a few of the men on the bench had actually heard the words and knew what had happened.

"There you are." At last Fog discovered the Duke, and together they sloshed across the Yard. The Duke was stirred by the incident. "Gosh, you should have seen him, Fog. He has everything, that bird. You ought to have seen him run over that last tackler. Believe me, the man's a football player. Look. There's a light in his room. He must be in."

They went up. McGuire was inside his room, feet on the desk in their favorite position, cigarette in his mouth. He was reading a small white booklet.

"Come in, gents. Come in and sit you down. I was just studying this valuable compendium of knowledge. Seen it?"

"What is the thing? Oh, the Freshman guide, yes, I've got my copy in my pocket now," said Fog. "It sure is a valuable addition to one's information on the educational setup in this vast institution."

"What is it?" The Duke glanced at the cover

of the white booklet in McGuire's hands. "Where'd you come by that?"

"It was sent to every freshman. An inside story on the different courses in each department, the lowdown on every instructor, tutor, and professor, in short the works. Everybody got one, you must have yours somewhere."

"No. At least I don't recall it. Here, let me have a look, Fog. No, I never received this thing. How did you get hold of it?"

"Seems to me it was sent to me at home just before I left New York. Wasn't yours, Mickey?"

"Uhuh. Came to me at home. Yours is probably there and hasn't been forwarded yet, Duke."

"More likely," said Fog, "his was never sent. The Duke comes from the West. They wouldn't recognize Waterloo, Iowa. Here at Cambridge, the west ends at Albany."

The Duke was reading it eagerly. "Say, look! Look what it says about Government 1. This is wonderful. 'Extremely valuable and every freshman who possibly can should make an effort to take it. Townsend lectures brilliantly and the course itself is a fine introduction to what is known as the lecture system as in effect at Harvard.' "

"Yep. That's right. I'll testify it's one great course," said Mickey. So far their conversation had been entirely on subjects academic. Neither of Mickey's friends cared to bring up the subject of the afternoon, although both were anxious to hear his side of the story in full. "But suppose you were an instructor, Duke." He grabbed Fog's copy from his pocket. "How'd you like this? 'Kennington, great authority but dull lecturer. Discourages many men who might otherwise love Spanish. Tends to close subject rather than illuminate it for the student.' "

"Or this." The Duke was now in the middle of the pamphlet. " 'Pratt, not very stimulating. Somewhat disorganized. Poor tutor.' Say. This must burn some of them up. How do you suppose they ever got their material?" he asked, skimming over the fifty pages of small print.

"I understand they questioned and cross-examined about half the freshman class last year and the year before. Held meetings and so forth to get their slant on the various courses and instructors."

"Well, it's hot. Get this. 'If you have any real love for music you can obtain benefit from the courses in that department. If on the other hand you are taking them to ease your schedule, you are making a grave mistake. In the first place they are none of them easy. In the second they require a knowledge of counterpoint. In the third they demand an enormous amount of reading and outside work.' "

"That's nothing. Here's the dope on the Department of Biology which must be fun for someone to read. 'The Department of Biology has had many years of existence as a separate department in the university, but few years without trouble. It has been unlucky from the start. For some reason bad luck has pursued it. There have been many upsets within the department from time to time, and it has had small help from without. Although it still struggles, it is having an uphill fight and has not attracted the sympathy of the authorities. Consequently it is one of the weakest of all departments at Harvard. Its chief defects are lack of a leader and the fact that it has been neglected by several successive administrations.' "

"Well, that pretty much tells the story. See what they say about my tutor, Moore, Duke."

"Let's see. Economics. Page 32. . . . Here it is. 'Get Moore if possible for a tutor. Live man.' Wonder how he lists my man, Davis."

"J. B. Davis?"

"No, Henry Davis, History. Here. 'H. G. Davis. Fair. Has a reputation of being a hard marker but knows stuff and can teach.' And listen to this, Mickey. This will hit you. 'Those men who are interested in athletics, journalism, or other extracurricular activities, should not forget this in planning their schedule. Be careful not to pile up too much work, especially the first half year. By all means do not take more than one laboratory course or attempt more than one extracurricular activity until after midyears in February. But try something. If not, you are likely to miss something that college has to offer. Those playing football should take only four courses the first half year and no other extracurricular activity until after midyears.' "

He stopped short. Suddenly he became aware that someone was at the open door. There were, in fact, three men standing politely on the doorsill. They remained, listening to his reading of the passage before they spoke. As he stopped and looked up, one of them, older and more assured, came forward and spoke. "Mr. McGuire?"

Mickey greeted them, beaming cordially. "Come in! Come right in. Glad to see you. Meet my two classmates, Mr. Smith and Mr. Wellington. This is Mr. Carson, the coach of the football team, and Mr. Rogers, the captain. I don't believe I know the other gentleman. . . ."

The third person, evidently an undergraduate, came forward and was introduced by the older man.

"Mr. Strong, manager of the team."

"Oh, yes, of course."

The Duke was stunned into speechlessness. The head coach and the captain of the varsity in Mickey's room. It wasn't enough that McGuire himself was a famous star, these celebrities had to show up. And they'd come on purpose to see Mickey, too. He knew well enough what they'd come about: the row that afternoon. News traveled fast. Imagine meeting the varsity coach your first month in college! Right where you could talk to him—that is if you had anything to say, which Jim hadn't. It was thrilling all right, he could write home to his father about it this evening. Mickey didn't seem thrilled, however; he kept grinning, but he was far from excited. To the hints and asides of the coach he was not overreceptive.

"Why, Mr. Carson, these gentlemen are my

closest friends. Anything you have to say you can say in front of them. No, Duke, stay here, Fog."

The older man was the more embarrassed of the two, if in fact he was not the most embarrassed man in the room. None of them were exactly at their ease. They shifted about in the hard chairs, they looked at each other, until at last the coach, a baldheaded, good-looking man, remarked,

"McGuire, we understand . . . h'm . . . that is we've been told there was some little trouble between you and head coach Jackson, of the freshman squad, at the field this afternoon. Now just what seems to have been the matter?"

Mickey's Irish face became bland and innocent. "Trouble? No trouble so far's I know."

The Duke and Fog looked at each other. Even the latter admired Mickey's independence and envied his coolness before these great personages. After all, the coach of the football team was the coach of the football team. The Duke watched intently. He also wondered what it was all leading up to and what would happen.

"Maybe I'm wrong. Set us straight, please. We heard there was some friction on the field today. These things happen now and again, and we want to clear the situation up." It was the captain talking. McGuire looked at him carefully as he spoke, saying nothing for a minute.

"What situation do you mean?"

"What made you turn your suit in?" The coach leaned forward in his chair. He was persuasive and earnest. "Now look here, McGuire, you'll help us all by telling us frankly what happened today. We want to get this thing straightened out for ourselves as well as for you. Men don't turn their suits in without some reason."

"Of course. Here's just what happened. I came down here from Andover as captain of last year's team. I realize that I'm only one of two hundred candidates, but after all I've played six years of football in school before I ever hit this place. The first day this week we had four or five teams scrimmaging. I didn't get into it. Second day, ditto. Third day, just the same. Today, still no chance. Until those teams get gummed up out there in midfield with neither making a yard against the other. Then he sends me in. Is that a square deal?" He looked round at the three men, who shook their heads.

"Today, on the fourth day's practice, and I

haven't had five minutes of scrimmage this year, the two first teams get deadlocked in midfield and the coach looks up at the crowd of us. 'McGuire, they . . . tell . . . me . . .' " and the Duke recognized his perfect imitation of the coach's voice. " 'They tell me you think you can play football. Get out there and let's see what you can do.' So I went out and showed him, that's all."

The head coach looked at the varsity captain and the captain looked at the manager. Then McGuire continued.

"Ask him or ask this man right here, ask Wellington if that's right. He was there and heard the whole thing. Now look at him. He's on the squad and hasn't had a chance to scrimmage yet. He comes from some school out there in the West, but maybe he's an All-American for anything the coach knows."

This was too much for the Duke. In a dry, cracked voice he explained: "Oh . . . I'm not. I . . . was an end on the high school team, that's all . . . we never even won . . ."

What it was they never won, the coach and captain didn't seem to care. The former interrupted, apparently not much interested in the Duke's ability or the record of his school.

"You see, Mr. McGuire . . ." but before the coach could finish the boy spoke.

"Just a minute, coach. All I ask is a square deal. If you think I got one down on that field, why, all right, skip it. I don't, so I'll skip it, too. I didn't come to college to play football. I came to get an education. I thought this college was the best place in the country and I still think so. If I play football, ok. If not, ok."

"Of course. That's an intelligent attitude and I think we all here understand and appreciate your feeling. We certainly don't want anyone, whether he's a former Andover captain or not, talked to like that on the field. Mr. Jackson is new on the job and doesn't know all there is to know about handling men. He made a mistake on you and is big enough to say so. Now we need you, McGuire, and we don't want any more trouble. If you come down to Soldier's Field tomorrow, I'm sure things will work out all right. Do me a favor, will you please?"

"Certainly, coach."

"Come down tomorrow afternoon for practice just as if nothing at all had happened."

"Sure. Why, sure, I'll come down." McGuire's alacrity surprised his classmates. But then, he was a surprising man. "Course I'll come down. And no hard feelings. A chance, that's all I want."

"You'll get it," said the head coach of the varsity, shaking McGuire by the hand. He smiled cordially at the Duke. It was a friendly, familiar smile, a smile that promised much, the contagious smile of an old acquaintance. But he did not bother to shake his hand. Nor did the captain nor the manager as they turned and went downstairs.

"Economics 4b," said McGuire, picking up the booklet from the desk. "Economics 4b, that's what I want to take next year. If I can pass Ec. 1, that is. What does it say about the profs. in that course, Duke?"

6

The Duke walked slowly back to the locker room in a contented frame of mind. It was getting dark and from behind the varsity fence he could hear the sound of kicked footballs and the last shouts of the coaches as their practice ended. For almost the first time that fall he felt entirely satisfied over his game. To be sure he was only playing on the fourth team, but anyhow he had been scrimmaging at last, scrimmaging for a week now. That afternoon he had played end. Played well. It wasn't so much the two interceptions of lateral passes or the fact that he'd tackled the opposing backs three times behind their lines for a loss, as the way he'd held up his side. No gains round his end, not in the whole forty minutes of scrimmage. He began to understand this waiting system of end play taught here. They wouldn't approve of it in the West, but he had to admit once you got the hang of it, the thing was effective. Darned effective.

Someone overtook him and, running past, slapped him on the back. In the dusk it was difficult to see the man's features, but the familiar swagger of the thick shoulders was recognizable. More so was the voice. "Hi there, Duke. Saw you making coupla swell tackles this afternoon." The two men trotting along beside the stocky figure turned and looked at him curiously. They were the first-string backs. McGuire's early season trouble had blown over. To some extent, that is. Neither the player nor the head coach addressed each other directly or pretended he had any great affection for the other person. The coach invariably managed to give orders to McGuire through one of his assistants. While McGuire never spoke to the coach and seldom referred to him directly by name. However, his place on the first team was assured. In fact it was obvious that he knew more football than anyone on the squad, and could be counted on to deliver his best game in the pinches. That he would be captain when the coaches finally gave their permission to the squad to elect a leader seemed fairly sure.

So the Duke went into the lockers swinging his headgear happily. Fourth team, to be sure, fourth team today, but in a week or so he'd be on the third eleven and before the Yale game a substitute. After all, he was no great player, he wasn't a world beater like McGuire. But he did want to get into the Yale game because he had to have his numerals. Father expected that and he couldn't go home Christmas without them. Back home he could wear his sweater turned inside out the way everybody did in Cambridge as if they were sort of ashamed of showing it. Naturally no one at home would know whether he was a first-string end or not. Except Father. He could tell his father; Father would be disappointed but understanding. The other fellows didn't matter. Already he was learning of their progress in letters from home. "Marshall Smith is playing on the freshman team at State." Or, "Eddie Mason has made the varsity at Grinnell." Well, that was all right, there wasn't the competition in those places there was here. Four big school captains all trying for the two end berths on the freshmen. Father would understand. He'd be satisfied.

Inside the freshman locker room the air was warm and pungent with the familiar odor, a mixture of sweaty bodies, dirty clothes, and the smell of unguents and ointments from the tables of the rubbers across the hall. One of the backs on the third eleven passed him on the way to the shower. "That was some tackle you made on me this afternoon. I just about had the ball away and we had a clear field for a touchdown, too." The Duke grinned as he sat down to undress. This crowd wasn't so bad when once you got to know them. They were different from the gang back home, that's all. More reserved and quiet and not so free and easy, but they were all right. He pulled off his hood, threw it on the floor and stooped down to unlace his shoes. Then he ripped off his pants, took off his socks and the stockings, and peeled his red jersey over his head. The hip pad took some time to undo, and then he threw off his undershirt, and tore off a bandage of tape around his leg. For the first time, except during that brief moment the evening of the riot, he began to feel part of this huge organism which was the university.

Someone was singing in the showers. There was the sound of splashing water and shouts across the room. He felt exuberant as the last bit of tape peeled away showing the bruise healthy and healing. Then his exuberance suddenly disappeared. He was tired, dead beaten, and there was that section meeting in History to prepare for the next morning. Back home Saturday was Saturday, here it was the day of his two section meetings, the hardest morning of the week. He reflected with a smile that out home football was different, too, and he remembered once when they had lost a game in school they had expected to win, that Mr. Barnes, the coach, got annoyed and painted on the seat of the quarterback's pants the warning: "If ahead do not pass."

Undressed, he went over to the weighing machines. 158. About four pounds underweight. Coolidge, one of the first-string ends, was right behind. The Duke watched as he stepped on the scales. 188. No, 190. He had a broad back and enormous shoulder muscles, a former halfback from Groton converted into an end and doing so well that he had displaced one of the two regular ends, both of whom were prep school captains. That showed the sort of competition one had to face here. He'd just tell this to Father in the next letter. No wonder the going was tough when you had to fight against birds like Coolidge.

The Duke stepped into the running shower, luxuriously enjoying the warm water against his back, his thighs, his stomach. He turned around twice and threw his head to one side so it could beat full on his arms and chest. Then he let it fall against the bruise on his leg, and soaping himself, stood under the spray. Hotter now, hotter. Wonderful. The best part of the day those moments under the shower.

Someone was waiting to get in for all the showers were full. He stepped out, dried himself, and went back to the rubbing room. "Well, Meester Wellington. Eh? Sure, we got plenty work tonight. Them first team boys they got all banged up this afternoon. Yah. Only Meester McGuire, he pretty tough, ha-ha."

So back to the lockers. What was that? As he came in he overheard snatches of a sentence passing back and forth between two men next to his locker. They talked in an undertone, but the last words were audible. "New rubbing list." A new rubbing list! No one had told him anything about that. Probably meant another cut in the squad. The last cut, and tomorrow some poor blokes wouldn't be playing—at least not on the freshmen. The man against him, for instance, that end on the other team. Hard luck, but life was like that. He hummed a tune and turned to dress. If only he hadn't had that accursed section meeting to work upon. The shower was refreshing, so was the rubdown, but he knew perfectly well that a dinner would make him so sleepy that by nine o'clock he would be unfit to concentrate upon the lives of the barons in medieval France. His section man was tough, too.

He dressed and handing his dirty clothes to the boy to go into the cleaner, shut his locker and looked around. Purse. Watch. Change. He was forever leaving things down there overnight. Shoving on his coat he left the warm room, went downstairs to the main door. There was a group standing beside the freshman notice board. Yes, there it was.

"Until further notice the following men will

constitute the freshman rubbing list. All others turn in equipment to Asst. Manager Paul K. Fields, Jr., tomorrow afternoon." Then came a long list of names and at the bottom another paragraph. "Dropped men are reminded that further facilities for football exist among the 150-pound teams and the teams of the various houses. These men are urged not to give up the game, as players who in the past failed to make the freshman squad have proved to be first-string varsity material in later years."

"Aw, nerts," said a boy in front of the group. He shoved carelessly past the Duke, a scowl on his face. It was the man who had played opposite end against him that afternoon. He turned and went out, the door slamming behind him with a bang.

The Duke edged nearer. His eye ran quickly down to the end of the list. There were a lot of W's on the freshman squad. Walsh. Williams. D. P. Winthrop. Winship. Woodward. Wyeth.

Someone next to him who had been dropped made a sour remark, but the Duke didn't exactly catch what he said, or care, either. No more football. How would he explain that to his father? Not even on the freshman squad. He stumbled to the door behind a laughing group of first-string players. As he stepped into the darkness a familiar hand reached out and grabbed him tightly by the arm. Someone in the rear called out to McGuire.

"No, thanks, Hubbard, I'm walking up with the Duke." It was the varsity captain condescending to ask McGuire to walk to the Square and McGuire was refusing. The varsity captain! Ordinarily, this would have made an enormous impression on the Duke. Not that evening.

7

The card under the door was brief. "YOU ARE REQUESTED TO REPORT TO THE DEAN OF FRESHMEN AT UNIVERSITY 4 ON TUESDAY NOVEMBER 16 BETWEEN TEN AND TWELVE."

That card puzzled him. The riot was now over and forgotten save by those unfortunate members of the class whose names had been taken and who had been summoned to the Dean to be placed on probation. Fog, an authority on the workings of the administration as on other subjects connected with the university, looked the card over with attention.

"Duke, I'm afraid you're really in for it. Somehow that proctor must have got your name when we rushed the Gate that night. They've probably just got round to the W's, see? It's hard luck, but it can only mean one thing."

McGuire disagreed. He knew too many men who were called to the Dean merely because they had neglected to give their father's middle name when they registered. It was nothing at all, that card. But the Duke felt otherwise. He agreed with Fog that it meant probation. Probation! First dropped from the football squad. Then probation because of that darned riot. What next? Yet somehow the more he thought of it the more he doubted even this explanation. There was, he felt, more to it than just the aftermath of the riot in the Square the previous month. So he was nervous and worried as he sat with half a dozen other dejected freshmen in the anteroom in University 4 that morning. The girl who summoned him in to the Dean was smiling and cheerful, however.

"Dean Henderson is away today. The assistant Dean is taking his place."

The assistant Dean was a young man with a suave manner who greeted him cordially. He had an enormous book open before him, its pages ruled off into squares and dotted with small marks in red. He turned the pages.

"Mr. Wellington. James H., Jr. That's right. You come from Iowa, don't you? H'm. Now let's see. Oh, yes. Did you—have any idea from your section men what your Hour Exam marks were, Mr. Wellington?"

So that was it! Those cursed Hour Exams. Just what he had been afraid of. The Hours had caught him badly prepared, and he hadn't even done himself justice in three of the five he had taken. Two of them were beyond him. In History his section head had made a warning gesture.

"Why, no . . . not exactly, that is . . ."

"Then you better take a look at them." The big book was shoved over toward him and he leaned above a blur of squared spaces, figures dancing before his eyes. Out of the page five red letters glared forth. C. D. E. E. E. Sweat suddenly came out on his forehead. He couldn't believe it. Three E's, a C, and a D.

"But . . . I thought . . . in French . . ."

"Well, there they are."

The Duke was staggered. Three E's, a C, and a D. Why, it wasn't possible. Surely he hadn't done as badly as that in History and French.

"What seems to be the trouble?"

"I don't know. I don't understand." He wiped the perspiration from his forehead, but the more he wiped the faster he perspired. "Those courses. I mean . . . I certainly thought I did better than that in French." Three E's, a C, and a D. Those couldn't be his marks.

"Do you work regularly? Have you been keeping up consistently all term? Perhaps you let yourself get behind? Or are you doing some sort of work outside, earning money or something?"

His face went red. He ought to be doing something like that, lots of fellows were and getting much better marks, too. "Why, no, I'm not doing any outside work at all."

"Did you try for the *Crimson?* Or are you out for football?"

"Yes, I played football—that is up to the last cut in the squad."

"When was that?"

"Let's see. October 30, I think." He didn't think; he knew. He'd never forget that date.

"Ah. That was the week before the Hour Exams. Did you find difficulty in keeping along up to that point?"

"I was always pretty tired at night, I know. Football sure does take it out of you. But I tried to work—to prepare for the Hours."

"Are you a slow reader?"

"Yes, I guess so. It seems to take me an awful long while to get through some of the reading assignments, in History, for instance." But those marks staring at him from the square ruled pages took all his attention. Three E's, a C, and a D!

"And English," the assistant Dean continued. "I note that you only just failed to get 75 in your entrance examination; that was unfortunate. You could have omitted English A had you got 75 in that examination and then you would only have had four courses on your hands. But 72 isn't a poor mark, yet you failed English A here. How does that happen? Spelling? Or do you write slowly?"

"Dunno. Both, I guess. Then those daily themes. They sort of get me down. I never had anything like that before."

"Well, Mr. Wellington, of course you realize this isn't exactly a creditable record. Ordinarily we don't have much mercy on a man who fails three courses at the November Hours. However, your adviser gives me a good report. He thinks the trouble in your case comes mainly from a difficulty in getting adjusted, in finding your feet. We do realize here that the change from school to college is enormous. I know things are very difficult. But you have certain things in your favor. The report of your adviser, the fact that you had a good record in school, and your honors in entrance examinations. Then you don't appear to have cut any classes, either."

The Duke hardly heard him. "I don't understand it. At school I never had any trouble. I was always up in the first ten, played football, basketball, and everything. But this place is so sort—sort of confusing."

"It is. So we are going to make an exception to one of our rules. Ordinarily three E's are sufficient to keep a man from continuing in college. But the Dean considers there must be something radically wrong with a man who gets honors in his entrance examinations and fails three of the Hours. So he intends to give you until Midyears to pull yourself out. Frankly, I know you can do much better, but whether you can raise those three E's I don't know. In English you certainly should improve your grade. And History—why, that was the subject you took honors in! Economics, of course, is a difficult subject. You've planned out a hard program, and now you have a job ahead. It's up to you."

"I . . . that is . . ." He didn't know what he was saying. What could anyone say faced with such remarks? His forehead continued to perspire embarrassingly.

"So we'll give you until Midyears then. That's understood, isn't it? It's evident you have a good mind and your adviser believes in letting you have every chance. I'm taking his word and so is the Dean. Keep in close touch with him, that's what he's here for. Naturally you appreciate you are on probation. That means no cutting, no participation in any extracurricular activities, and implies a strict attention to work. Otherwise there's nothing more I can say. Let me know— or the Dean, he will be back next week—let either of us know if we can be of assistance. And good luck." He rose and held his hand out. The Duke took it, turned, and went from the room, his face red as he passed by the waiting group outside. The November sunshine in the Yard almost blinded him, and a cold wind cut his perspiring forehead. His legs felt weak at the knees, as if he had been hit by a blocker when playing football. Three E's, a C, and a D, he kept repeating. Three E's, a C, and a D. He walked across the Yard, up the three flights of stairs, and stumbled into the room. Three E's, a C, and a D.

The goody was cleaning up, banging and fussing around with the vacuum cleaner. Yes, he'd rather she came back later on. Three E's, a C, and a D. It just wasn't possible! But it was possible. No use hedging or fooling himself. He was a failure at college. First football, now this. Three E's, a C, and a D. Why, he must be almost the lowest man in the class. Stubbornly thoughts of home came to him, of his father standing on the platform, of the band, of the fellows grouped round, of old Mr. Phillips handing him the watch. There it was now on his wrist. He took it off and threw it as hard as he could across the room.

His head sank onto the desk. From below there came a full-chested shout. "Duke. Hey, Duke!" Only McGuire after the History notes. He didn't want to see him. McGuire, captain of the freshman team, the man who found everything so simple, who skimmed through History and other courses as easily as he breezed down the field with a returned punt. No, just then the Duke wished to be absolutely alone.

But the door flew open.

"What's up?" McGuire stood in the doorway looking at the dejected figure in the chair. "What's happened to you, Duke?"

The Duke didn't raise his head. Through his arms came the words, "Three E's, a C, and a D."

"What?" Even McGuire's customary composure was rocked. "Three E's, a C, and a D. Boy!"

Coming in, he shut the door carefully. The chapel bell clanged vigorously and McGuire had an important section meeting at eleven o'clock, but he stayed in the room. "So that's what the call to the Dean was about." No answer. "Well, so what?" He waited and still there was no answer. "How long has he given you?"

"Until Midyears."

"Midyears. Well, you got two months yet. Two months is two months. C'm on now. . . ."

"Yeah, but you don't understand. My father . . . he's been looking forward to all this, to my coming here for years. How can I go back home now for Christmas? How can I, huh? A failure, that's what I am. Kicked off the football team, didn't even make the squad. How can I explain that to the folks home, to Father and everyone who had me an All-American end? Then probation. Three E's, a C, and a D. What can you do with a record like that?"

"Listen. Forget you're going home. Forget all that business of your father. All you gotta do is to get out of the trenches by Midyears."

"With three E's, a C, and a D to work on?"

"Sure. What of it. Marks don't matter. The Hour Exam marks don't count much if you have a good record the rest of the term. How do I know? My tutor told me so last week. Mason told me you can pull 'em up, kid. You're gonna pull 'em up. For the next two months we're gonna work, you and I. Yep, both of us. Like we never worked before. My marks? I don't know what they were, but they weren't any too good from the way several section men spoke to me. I'm in danger."

"That's all right for you to say. But what can anyone do with three E's, a C, and a D? I'm disgraced and I've disgraced Father. I can't go home. Guess I'd better get a job and go to work. You don't understand."

"Don't I? So you think. Listen. I went through

the same thing three years ago at Andover. Same thing you're going through right this minute. I came up there a junior from Natick High. You never heard of Natick, did you? Well, Natick produced some of the best football men that ever came to this place. Mahan, Casey, he was coach a while back, and a lot of others. But going from Natick to Philips Andover is like going from your school out there in Iowa to Harvard. I came up with a big rep and fell down. Didn't even make the football team. Why? Dunno, guess I thought I knew all there was to know about football. I was only a substitute the first fall. Then I failed badly at Midyears and the principal invited me to leave. Said I wasn't what he called college material, whatever that means. Said I'd never get into Harvard in a hundred years. Said I wouldn't even get through the term. Oh, yeah, says I. My Irish was up. I worked that winter, day and night. Learned what it was to concentrate. Well . . . I got by. Finally. Came in here with honors last fall. So what? So this. If I could do that three years ago as a kid, you can do it now at your age."

"D'you really think so? Those marks . . ."

"Forget 'em. Forget 'em all. Just get busy and

work." He walked across the room, picked up the watch from the floor, listened to it, and handed it over to the Duke.

"Now stop being a child. Put this on and get busy. First of all, that History had you down, didn't it? All right. Let's see where you stand on the reading for this week."

8

Mr. Wellington drove into the garage, pulled on the brake, shut off the motor, and turned out the lights. It was half-past five and dark as he prepared for the difficult business of removing himself, first from the car and then from the garage. "These new models are the devil and all to get out of," he muttered, squeezing himself through the door and into the narrow space between the car and the wall of the garage.

"Well, Mother." He came into the lighted

kitchen, and saw her agitated face. "Good heavens, what's up?"

"I've had a letter from James." Her voice was frightened and so was her look as she glanced at the sheets of paper in her hands.

"What's the matter? Is he sick?"

"No. He isn't coming home for the Christmas vacation."

"Not coming for Christmas? I thought he had the flu at least, way you looked when I came in."

"I know, but I don't like it at all. He says he thinks he ought to stay in Cambridge to study. That doesn't sound like James. Here, you read his letter." Mr. Wellington put on his glasses, took the typewritten pages and held them under the kitchen light.

DEAR FATHER AND MOTHER,

After some thought I've decided not to come home for the Christmas vacation after all. Of course this is a big disappointment to me. I was looking forward to getting back and I know you will be disappointed, also. But work has been piling up pretty fast during the football season. Football not only took me all afternoon, but usually left me too tired to do much real work at night and I put off a lot of stuff I should have done early in the term. This got me behind in two courses and I think it's best to stay and make up some of the back reading here in the library. They sure do expect a man to get through a lot of work here. For instance, in History this week the assigned reading was a book of twelve hundred pages on feudalism in the middle ages. Hard reading, too. I'll be pretty lonesome on Christmas Day. But on the whole it seems to me best to stay right here and work. Please give my regards to Eddie and Jim. I sent a card to Marshall Smith and Mary Parsons. Tell Spot, old boy, I'll be back after the Midyears. We have almost two weeks' vacation at that time. Your loving son.

P.S.—If Dad wants to give me something I could use this Christmas I wish he would let me buy a secondhand typewriter, I rented this one.

Mr. Wellington closed his glasses and put them into the case with a snap. "Well, Mother, what makes you worry over that letter? I don't see anything special to get excited about. Seems he's finding the going harder than we expected. I remember he always did have trouble doing his reading and maybe they pile it up there at Cambridge. That advanced French course, too much for him, I imagine. . . ."

"Yes, I know, but it doesn't seem just right to me. He was always so fond of Christmas at home. I do hope he isn't getting into trouble of some kind."

"Now, Mother, what kind of trouble would he get into? Jim's a good boy."

"Oh, I know, that's what worries me. Maybe he isn't well. Or maybe he's been playing poker. You know you spoke to him about playing poker last year, or was it the year before? Or maybe he wants to be near some girl there or something."

Mr. Wellington laughed. "What if he does? Maybe he has been playing poker. I played poker at his age in college. Why shouldn't he play, now he's in college? I didn't want him playing in high school, that's all. If he loses his money he'll just have to make the best of things. I think he's telling the truth, things came easy in high school, but now he's in another world. Imagine he's having a hard time with the changeover, but he'll come out all right. I wouldn't worry about him if I were you. Just let him plan things the way he thinks best. Besides," and the prudent businessman was speaking, "if he doesn't come home that'll save two hundred dollars. Not that I wouldn't like mighty well to see the boy again," added the father. "This house seems like a tomb since last September."

The telephone rang. His wife went into the hall and he heard her voice as she answered, noticed it change tone when the conversation went along. "Hullo. Oh, good evening, Mary. How's your mother? I've been meaning to run in to see her, but I've been so busy this week. She is? I'm so glad. Yes, we're all just fine, too. Oh, he seems to be all right. Uhuh, we had a letter this afternoon. What's that? When? Christmas week? No, Mary, I'm afraid he couldn't. He isn't coming home at all this vacation. No, he thinks he must stay there and work. We only heard this afternoon. Yes, we're disappointed, too, but his father is very philosophical about it. Well, Jim says he got behind in his reading during the football season. He always was such a slow reader. Yes, otherwise he's fine and seems to be enjoying himself. What's that? Well, I believe he made the freshman team, we never heard much about it, he is so bad in his letters. I think he said they lost to the Yale freshmen, that was all. Give my love to your mother, Mary. Good-bye." She turned to her husband. "That was Mary Parsons. Wants him for a dance Christmas week. A fortnight before he sets foot in town; really, the way these girls pester the boys nowadays . . ."

Back in Cambridge the Duke was studying. To be sure he had studied before. He had prepared for examinations in high school, plugged for the College Board, and he felt he knew something about work. But never had he worked as he worked during that next six weeks. Luckily McGuire was in two of his courses and Fog in the other three, so each night one of them came to his room to cover the ground with notes and books. As McGuire remarked, thoroughness was essential. So the Duke devoted his afternoons to getting up and keeping up his current work, to writing that infernal daily theme, to reading in the library.

Outwardly he was driven and kept at it by his

friends, both determined he was not going to fall down in his courses. He was also driven inwardly. The thought of returning home a failure was something he didn't dare consider. Sometimes he would wake up at night in an awful dream in which he was coming into the Sycamore Street station, his father on the platform holding Spot on a leash. Even Spot had a reproachful look on his fuzzy face. Then he would wake up in a terrifying sweat.

"You see," he explained to McGuire, "my dad has been thinking of this and planning for it ever since I can remember. He sort of lives through his college days again. Been saving and working to give me this for years and years. Harvard, that's all I've heard for goodness knows how long. You fellows here in the East sort of take it as a matter of course—"

"Not me, I don't. Those friends of Fog's, maybe—"

"That's what I mean. The bunch that comes here gets to expect it. But out our way it's a big thing, to come East for an education. Not so many do and when you have a chance they expect something of you. Dad does, I know. He expected me to make the freshman team.

He expects me to make the clubs. I know I won't—"

"How do you know you won't? Besides, what do you care about that bunch of drunks?"

"Don't you understand, it isn't me, it's Dad. He's been thinking and planning about this for ten or fifteen years now. I can't let him down, and by gosh I'm not going to either."

That was the one thought which spurred him on and kept him going. It made him work as he had never worked before, opened up an entirely different concept of effort to his imagination. Not a moment of the day could be wasted if he hoped to accomplish what the Dean said was improbable, if not impossible. Time counted. Time was sacred, to be dished out sparingly, to be utilized to the full. In the morning he dragged himself from bed at eight-thirty to the sound of the alarm clock. A bath, a shave, and he jumped into his clothes. Then he spilled some dirty brown powder into a cup, poured hot water from the faucet over the mess, and drank it. This was called cocoa. A dash across the Yard to a nine o'clock. All morning he was at lectures or section meetings. Evenings he worked with one of his friends, and then continued alone until he fell asleep over a pile of books at one or later in the morning.

Later on in college other problems arose, but nothing that could ever be compared to the trial by fire of the first half year at Cambridge.

9

The endless prairies of southern Iowa rolled past the windows of the Pullman while the Duke sat balancing things. A year ago, no, a thousand years ago, he had sat in the same seat and on the same train, had passed the same scenery for Cambridge. What about it? Well, those hopes seemed pretty foolish twelve months later. He had really fallen down in every one of his father's expectations. First, he'd been unable even to make the freshman football squad, let alone the team. That meant no chance for the varsity even if he went out, which he had no intention of doing. His two roommates were certain to be chosen for the clubs. Mickey because of football, Fog because of his friends. No, that was unkind. Fog would be chosen because he was Fog. Because he was J. Faugeres Smith of Groton and Hewlett, Long Island. But more especially because he was a darn good guy. The sort of person everyone liked to be with. He knew more men than anyone in the class. The Duke hardly knew a dozen, and no one knew him. How could you expect prominence when you'd never done anything? He was a cipher, just a member of the sophomore class, another undergraduate.

There were things on the credit side, however. It was true, he was going to disappoint the old man badly. That was certain. Even his father was vaguely aware of it, and the subject of clubs, of undergraduate success had not been mentioned this last summer as it had the summer before. But anyhow he was going to have a much better time than as a freshman. Serious application counted. His marks had come up, way up. In the finals, although he had not done himself justice, he was right up with Fog and not far behind Mickey who was a genius for taking examinations. Also, he had the two best roommates in the class, and because he was rooming with Mickey he had a suite overlooking the river in Dunster which was cheaper than his single room in the Yard. This year he wouldn't be lonesome and homesick, at least.

A good room and two fine roommates. That was something. Which one did he like best? Hard to tell. As the term started and they all three got settled into Dunster H 35, he found he enjoyed them equally, both the Boston Irishman and the Groton man from Long Island. As two of the best-known men in the class, their room was usually full all day with all kinds of visitors. Fog's friends, he found, frequently embarrassed him. Mickey's friends were different. They were nearly always Irish, invariably poor, sometimes athletes and seldom scholars. Marvelous fellows, like Mickey they appeared to study at rare intervals, but were never at a loss for a quick answer in classes or section meetings, and apparently able to meet the instructor on equal terms. Examinations to them were a joy and not a dreadful ordeal. Like Mickey they had a fine distaste for the conventions and formalities of university life and made no bones about saying so to anyone who listened. The Duke liked them and they liked him, calling him "Duke" the first time they met him and making him feel warm and comfortable.

The men who came to see Fog were different. They were mostly his classmates at Groton or from St. Paul's or some preparatory school, who knew each other well. They were usually wealthy although they gave no sign of wealth, seldom athletes, invariably active in some form of undergraduate life like the *Crimson*, and as often as not scholars. They worked, and the background of their work was visible. They had an ironical detachment about life and the university which the Duke envied and wished he could emulate. Their manners left nothing to be desired. They met the host and his roommates with charm and ease. The Duke liked them and didn't like them. This queer business of knowing a man one minute and not knowing him an hour later in the Yard took some getting used to. He spoke about it one evening when he was alone with McGuire.

"Oh . . . that crowd," replied the Irishman,

dismissing them contemptuously. "Fog's all right, but that crowd of his . . ."

Yet the Duke was always embarrassed in their presence. He never seemed able to engage in their chatter, half the time he did not know what they were talking about. A mystery to him, the names of the shows they attended or the dances in Boston upon which they bestowed their favors. They were working as assistant managers of teams, running for the *Lampoon*, and leading gay lives in town, yet they were all able to hold their own and more in their work. A dazzling and a distressing crowd.

Probably that was the reason he got into the thing at all. They were in the room late one night, half a dozen of them, attempting to kid Mickey, which was not the most profitable proceeding in the world.

"You're actually getting fat, Mickey," someone remarked. "Have to take off some weight or you'll never make the varsity this fall."

"I'll take my chance. Can still outrun any of you gents right this minute."

"I'd like to see you really run. Really run, not run down the field with a couple of interferers ahead of you."

"Run!" McGuire was touched. His pride was at stake. "Run! Why, I'll run from here to Wakefield and kick a football all the way before you fellows get back to Cambridge from a dance at the Somerset."

"You would, would you? Wakefield is about twelve miles. I'd like to bet $25 you couldn't kick a football between Wakefield and the Square from, say, three in the morning until the bell rings for the nine o'clock."

"H'm . . . I'd take you up . . ." He was an Irishman, but he was cautious . . . "I'd take you up only that History section meeting . . . just wait another month, will yuh?"

They started to jeer. This irritated the Duke. He happened to know Mickey was uncertain about his work in History and actually paying attention to the reading. So from a corner of the room he spoke. The sound of his own voice startled him. So did the words.

"Of course he could. Why, anyone in good training could do that."

They turned on him. That quiet, western fellow, what was his name? Why did Fog happen to room with an egg like that? "All right. The bet's still good. Let's see you grab it."

"I will."

"You will?" Now the entire room gave him their attention.

"Can you run?"

"You can't run."

"Who ever told you that you could run?"

"Duke . . . you ought to have your head examined." Their derision was unanimous and instantaneous. Except for Mickey and Fog. But he stuck to it.

"Never said I could run. I just said I'd take up that $25 that I can kick a football from Wakefield to the Square between three in the morning and the time the bell rings for the nine o'clock."

"Sounds like easy money to me. I'll put up ten, Henry. Phil, you take five, will you? If you want something soft, you better get in on this, Bill. . . ."

"I'll take fifteen bucks of the Duke's money." McGuire to the rescue. "I happen to think he can do it."

"Thanks, Mickey. I want all of this myself. Now, let's settle the details. From Wakefield to the Square, that's about twelve miles, in six hours. Of course we'll have to use a soccer ball. That's all right with you?"

"Sure. A soccer ball. When do we start?"

They started exactly at three the next morning from the center of Wakefield Common. George Preston with whom he had made the bet rolled him out in his car, and two other cars followed, carrying interested friends. Mickey placed the ball on the ground and kicked off as a big clock on the town hall struck the first note of three o'clock.

The April morning was not warm, and at first the Duke's hands and feet were numb. He wore a pair of running pants, a sweatshirt, his skiing boots, and the two thickest wool socks he could buy. Nervously slapping his body with his arms he wondered why he had ever taken up the crazy bet at all. Well, $25 was $25. His whole month's allowance. Where he'd find money to pay up if he lost he couldn't imagine. So he wouldn't worry about that but simply go out and win.

They started with George and two of his friends in a car ahead, Mickey with Fog in the roadster behind, and a third car filled with two more men and extra soccer balls in the rear. The constable watched them for a few minutes from the shadow of the A. & P. store in the center of town, and then let them alone. Just a bunch of boys training for the B.A.A. marathon.

The light on the car behind kept the road in plain view and enabled him to kick the ball on one side of the road. For the first few miles from Wakefield he progressed at a comfortable trot. Gradually his feet tingled, then warmed up, and after a mile his hands and his body were warm and he felt able to breast a cold wind which was rising. The direction led down Main Street straight for almost eight miles, past sleeping commuters in houses, closed stores, and black shop windows. A traffic cop on a motorbike whirled by, slowed down, and looked the group over suspiciously, then quickened his speed and roared on, leaving a nasty smell from his exhaust. Cheers, groans, and shouts of all kinds came from the cars ahead and behind. At any rate they were enjoying the trip.

Main Street still, he observed by a sign under an arc light. There was a Main Street at home. Must be a million Main Streets in the United States. He caught up with the ball and shoved it ahead doggedly. By the time they'd covered a couple of miles he found himself using his left foot to give his right one a rest. That procedure had disadvantages. The trouble was he couldn't control the ball so well. At times it skirted off at right angles across the road. Or into front yards, because the cursed thing had a genius for finding an open gate or an embankment in a field below. That meant effort to get it out as he was not allowed to use his hands. At Stoneham Center he slowed down and walked through the town. Already the pace was beginning to tell on him.

Big trucks loaded with market produce en route to the city rolled along. A clock struck four. Three miles in an hour. Good time, yes, but the thing was only starting. He quickened his speed and at Spot Pond, a mile and a half further along, that ball which at first was a light balloon had become as heavy as dough. The cheers, jeers, and shouts from the cars were now stilled. Watching the endless trot and kick, trot and kick, tired them almost as much as it did him. The cavalcade came into Melrose in silence for by this time some of the occupants of the cars were nodding.

The first casualty occurred as they turned off the Fellsway. A wild kick to the left, the glare of approaching headlights, an explosion, and a deflated piece of pigskin lying on the road. The cars came to life with delight. Another ball was tossed out and the procession continued.

Medford at five-thirty. He was safe if he could only keep it up at that pace. But he was tiring, the wind was coming up all the time, and the going was tougher. His dog-trot was now half a walk and half a run, and at times he found he was walking up to the ball so that he got little force into the kick. This made it necessary to hit the ball more often. Traffic, too, was increasing. By six, when it was light, there seemed to be no end of the hooting, shrieking cars that roared along carrying early morning workers into the city, their faces against the windows as they went past the strange group.

They stopped for a traffic light at Broadway in Medford and Mickey jumped out of the front car.

"Can you make it, kid? How you feel?"

"Aw'right. Tired. . . ."

"Stick to it. George has just taken ten more with Bill you won't do it. Course you can. Here, try some of this brandy."

He gulped on the brandy. The traffic lights changed. Cars behind honked impatiently, so with a determined punch at the ball he moved along. By this time the thing felt like a punching bag.

Ball number two was sacrificed at the entrance to Somerville. Apparently the whole town was at work before eight in the morning, and the going was slow. At last they reached the long, straight stretch of Kirkland Street with hardly two miles to home. Fog, who was timing them, jumped out and ran alongside. "Forty minutes, Duke, old boy. You better step on it. Only a couple of miles to go. Give 'em everything you got."

Yes . . . but suppose you had nothing left. Suppose the road lay endless ahead. At his feet was that accursed ball, the ball which always seemed to be there waiting. His legs were like iron, so tired he could hardly feel them except when he hit out. Then he felt them all right, felt them with shoots of pain down to his ankles. He had worked through the toes of both socks, and there were terrible blisters on each foot. Why had he been such a fool as to speak up? All right for the birds in the car to tell him to give everything he had, but they hadn't kicked that thing from Wakefield.

Now the traffic going toward Boston was a steady flow, with a constant roar in his ears. Two more balls were run over and lost, delaying them.

He wondered, almost without caring, whether there were any more left. Then far off in the distance above the rooftops he saw the tower of Memorial Hall. Almost there. Only a mile or so now!

"Hurry, Duke, old kid. Hurry now, put everything you've got into it. You can just make it. Don't quit now you have these birds cold. They never thought you could do it." That last sentence encouraged him. While from the car ahead the cries and shouts assured him his chances were hopeless. "Better quit, boy. You can never make it now. Not a chance. Why not hop in for the rest of the ride. We'll slow up for you . . . see. . . ." He paid no attention to them, lowered his head and charged at the ball which by now was as heavy as a medicine ball. And no more manageable. Memorial at last! The big gold clock showed ten to nine. The whole thing might hinge on a missed traffic light.

Across the Delta, then legs aching intolerably, breath gone, he stood panting on the curb until he could work through the incessant line of cars. The rest of the crowd was at his heels, while groups of students were passing over to the New Lecture Hall for a nine o'clock. He heard their amazed comments. "What's doing? Hey, what's the idea? No . . . it's that man kicking a soccer ball from Wakefield on a bet. That's McGuire, the quarterback, behind him . . ."

Across the street. Then inside the gate to the Yard where he saw Bill and George Preston waiting. They were unfurling something, some kind of a banner. As he entered they stepped ahead, hoisting the banner by two long poles. It had a savage crack on it, but he was too tired to read it or care. They were going to make him earn his money; well, let them. The steps of University where he was to finish were packed, and there was a large crowd in front who greeted his appearance with a roar. He gave the ball a desperate kick, trying to outdistance the standard-bearers up front, but the strength was gone from his legs and he could hardly push it forward.

"The last hundred yards are the hardest," yelled someone in the crowd. They were all yelling. He didn't hear what they said as he shoved that ball with his ankles, his legs, and his knees up to University, past the steps, and over the line. He fell on the ground, or would have fallen down if Mickey, running up, hadn't caught him. The clock on Memorial bonged out the hour and the bell on Harvard began its shrill call to classes.

Mr. Wellington heard the news that afternoon in Waterloo when a friend came in and left the evening edition of the *Courier* on his desk. The Associated Press reported the story from its Boston correspondent under the headline, "Home Town Boy Wins Bet. James H. Wellington, Jr., son of James H. Wellington of Ottumwa Power and Light and a sophomore at Harvard, won a large bet today, reported to be several hundred dollars, from his friend and classmate, George Preston, Jr., son of George Preston, president of the Bankers Trust Company of New York, by kicking a football twelve miles from Wakefield, Mass., to Harvard Square in six hours. The story of the bet was related in this morning's Harvard *Crimson,* and a large crowd gathered in front of University Hall to see the end of this race against time which ended with a minute to spare just before nine this morning. Young Wellington was a member of the freshman football team last year and is a popular student in the second year class."

Luckily for his peace of mind, young Wellington did not see the story in the *Courier* for several months. His feet bandaged, he was fast asleep in his room in Dunster, sleeping through his classes for almost the first time since he had entered college.

10

Obviously it was Fog's idea from the start. No one except Fog could have conceived it and no one but Fog could have executed it and carried it through to completion.

They were sitting in their room one winter afternoon overlooking the frozen river, Fog reading the *New York Times* to which he subscribed and which he read carefully every day. The Duke, his feet on the fireplace, was doing some required reading in History 22 which both his roommates took and in which neither ever seemed to do any work. On the front page of the *Times* was a short account of the impending visit of the President to Cambridge. His son was about to be made a member of the Fly, and the President had decided to come on the following week for his initiation which coincided with the hundredth anniversary of the founding of the club. Fog tossed the paper to the floor and sat looking out the window.

"Maybe . . . maybe . . . yessir, that's an idea. No . . . we couldn't work it from here. Wait a minute. Mickey, do you know anything about radio?"

From the bedroom Mickey, who was on his bed reading, answered, "Not a thing."

"H'm. Do you, Duke?"

The Duke glanced up. His mind was as far as possible from radio and modern sciences. "Why, yes . . . in a sort of way, I suppose. Rather as an amateur of course. Why?"

"How much do you know, really?"

He put his book aside. "Oh, I had the craze, same as every kid. Built myself a homemade radio and sat up half the night trying to get Australia when I was in school. It was a hobby that I kept up a little through High and so they made me president of the club. Didn't amount to much, though we used to think so. Why? What's on your mind?"

"Never mind. You understand the principles? Of loud speakers and all that sort of thing, I mean?"

"Why, of course. But what's all the shooting about?"

"Come along." He rose, shoved on his coat and tossed over the Duke's. Downstairs he ran, two steps at a time. Across De Wolfe, up Plympton. By his quick strides the Duke realized something pretty important was on. "Hey, what's the rush, Fog? I have to finish those three hundred pages by tonight." But his roommate was too preoccupied to answer. In fact, he was so preoccupied he almost got himself run over in crossing Holyoke Street, and then collided with a figure coming out of the archway into the quadrangle of Lowell. Opposite was the main entrance to the building, with the white-topped tower above. Fog rushed in, and up the stairs. At the third story there was a small door marked "Tower." He pushed. It was locked. Taking out a bunch of keys, he tried one after the other. The third one opened the door. They went in.

It was cold and damp inside the tower. A narrow flight of steps led round and gradually up to the bell chamber on top where were the famous Lowell Bells, brought from England and presented to the House by the former president of the University. They were in the peak of the tower now, several hundred feet above the ground, with a superb view of the smoky, snow-covered roofs of Cambridge. Across the river stood the stadium, bleak and bare. Beside and below and all about were the Houses grouped together: Dunster to the east, then Winthrop, Eliot, and Kirkland, while across Mt. Auburn Street were the queer contours of the Lampoon building. But Fog was paying no attention to the view. Instead he was leaning over the parapet looking down attentively on the small brick building which nestled in the shadow of the tower. That building was the home of the Fly Club.

"H'm. Of course we'd need plenty of warm clothing. Here an hour or more. But we can do it. By golly, we can do it."

"Do what, Fog? What's it all about?"

"You'll see, boy. Before the end of next week we'll make history around this place."

The day of the President's visit was cold and snowy. By nightfall, several inches of snow lay on the ground, yet this had failed to deter a crowd which gathered to await his arrival. For this was an event. A great occasion. Presidents don't come on from the White House for a club dinner very often. When his special train pulled into the Allston yards at seven, the streets round the Houses and the little square in front of the Fly Club were filled with cold, feet-stamping humanity. Meanwhile, the Duke, Fog, and Mickey were perched in the upper tower of Lowell, getting a fine picture of the mob stretching up and down Mt. Auburn Street below. It was a solid mass of overcoated men and women, so crowded they could hardly move, flowing into the adjoining streets and pressing down from Massachusetts Avenue.

In a minute or two, three cars came poking their way down Mt. Auburn Street through the mob. The cheers became louder as they came slowly beneath the tower and stopped at the entrance to the Club. The President wore an overcoat but no hat and the fringe of snow about his head made him look white-haired. He stood on the steps of the building for a minute, waved to them, acknowledged their cheers which increased as he faced the crowd, turned, and went inside. The party followed, all except half a dozen secret service men who remained on guard at the door.

"All right, Duke?" In the cold of the open tower the Duke was fumbling with numbed fingers at a large amplifier. "Okay, Fog."

Fog stood in front of a portable microphone connected with the amplifier. "All right. Let her go, then." He was the leader, the one in command. At his word the surprised crowd below were startled by Mickey's voice from the heavens.

"Station L-O-W-E-L-L. Good evening, folks. This is your announcer, Graham McPhoney, and the Dunster Funsters bringing you a special plate-by-plate broadcast of the Fly Club celebration here tonight in Cambridge." For just a minute there was stunned silence below. Then the undergraduates in the crowd got the idea and cheered. They had located the voice in the Lowell Tower, and knowing the rivalry between Dunster and Lowell, guessed immediately that something was happening. To hear better they pressed forward. Noticing this movement, the Duke turned up the volume of the amplifier. Immediately up and down Mt. Auburn Street, into the lighted windows of Leverett and Lowell and Eliot, over the packed streets leading from the Drive, rose Mickey's sturdy voice. Now he was the perfect, unctuous announcer.

"Ladies and Gentlemen, the Dunster Funsters have the privilege of bringing you this special plate-by-plate broadcast of the hundredth anniversary of the founding of the historic Fly Club. A celebration which the President of the United States, himself a member of this club as an undergraduate, has seen fit to honor with his presence. We wish to thank Station L-O-W-E-L-L and the Lowell Bellringers for so kindly giving up their Itsy Bitsy Kiddie Hour and thus enabling the Dunster Funsters to describe for you this thrilling occasion. Before we go any further I will turn the microphone over to Ted Hooey who will give you this momentous plate-by-plate description of what takes place inside the Fly clubhouse on which we are now looking. All right, Ted, take it away." The mob below broke into cheers. This was something like. They hadn't anticipated it.

"Thank you, Graham McPhooey."

"And thank you, Ted Hooey."

"And thanks to you, Graham."

"But I thanked you first, Ted."

"Well, anyway, thanks, and thanks also to the broadcasting authorities of Lowell House and Station L-O-W-E-L-L and the Lowell Bellringers for letting us give this broadcast, and thanks to the Fly Club for installing a special skylight in their roof, thus enabling us to present to you one of the most thrilling, the most epic-making, the most—" Fog was in his element and enjoying himself, and his voice showed it—"the most, well, the greatest moment in American history. Think of it, folks, a president has come all the way from the White House in Washington to allow the Dunster Funsters to describe this event, and you, too, can tell your grandchildren that you took part at this stupendous affair. Well, from our point of vantage up here we can look right down into the Fly Club below and tell you just what's going on. Yes, the President's taking off his coat. Yes, he's definitely taking off his coat. Definitely. He is taking off his coat. No question about it now. I can see. Now he's shedding his galoshes. Yes, folks, and now he's shaking hands with all the members of the club. There are about two hundred in there, and they're all in evening clothes."

By this time a commotion was going on in the street below. Policemen were pushing through the crowd and stern voices crying, "Stop that up there," were greeted by jeers and hoots from the undergraduates present. The Duke leaned away from the amplifier and whispered to Mickey: "They'll be up any minute now. Better run down and hold that bolt on the lower door as long as you can. When it starts to give, jump back and run up here and lock the upper door."

Meanwhile, Fog's elegant tones continued without a second's pause. He was in his element. In his best announcerese, he went on. "Yes, sir, folks, this sure does promise to be a tremendous occasion for the Fly Club. What a crowd! What a dinner! O Boy, O Boy, O Boy, what a dinner! Looks like a Blue Plate Special from where I sit. Fit for a king. I mean a President. M'mmmmm . . . say, wouldn't I like to have some of those bottles of champagne they're passing round. Can't see the labels from here . . . no, wait till I get out the old glasses. It's Pol Roger. No, it isn't . . . yes, it is. No! It's Veuve Clicquot.

"Course all you folks know the President's son is going to be initiated tonight. That's it. That's one of the reasons why the President traveled all the way up from Washington, that and the fact that the Dunster Funsters arranged for this broadcast specially for you people eight years ago. Now then. Wait a minute. They're ready. In a second you'll hear the umpire's whistle. When you hear the gong strike it will be . . . I mean when you hear the whistle blow it will be toasting time in the Fly Club." He paused, and a long whistle manipulated by the Duke broke into the dialogue. The crowd below roared. They were enjoying themselves. Instead of dispersing after the President entered the clubhouse, they were standing in the cold eagerly waiting to see and hear what was going on. Every window in the Houses across the way was up, with occupants, their overcoats on, listening.

"There it goes. There it goes! It's a honey. Oh, boy, what a honey that toast was. I think it was sherry. No, it was port. Champagne, that's right, it was champagne. I was right the first time. Upsy-daisy. Upsy-daisy. Attaboy, Mr. President. Have another? No? Says he won't. He guesses he won't have another. Maybe they'll give a snooter to the secret service men out there on the porch. They sure do look as if they needed something." This sally brought a roar from the crowd. The mob in the street could see the unfortunate secret service detachment stamping their feet and waving their arms on the porch of the club.

"And who's that? It can't be? It is, yes, it's Colonel Charlie Apted himself, the crack water-pistol marksman and head of the Harvard police, the local Mounties." Here he was interrupted by shrieks from the undergraduates in the crowd. Colonel Apted, the Superintendent of Buildings, was not a heroic figure in undergraduate circles. With perfect timing, Fog let the applause die away. Then he went on in his gushing tone. "Yes, Colonel Apted has distinguished himself countless times in his adventurous career in the Yard here in Cambridge. He's peeping round the corner now with his large .45 caliber revolver in his hand." Cheers from below. The Colonel was well known. "But now we must get back inside and see exactly what's been going on.

"They're being seated. Yep, the whole gang is being seated at table. I can't tell who's next to the President. It looks like a college man. Well, anyway, they've started to eat. The President is going after an oyster. What technique!

It's on the end of his fork now. There she goes. Down the hatch, Mr. President. No . . . he dropped the darn thing in his lap. He's trying another. This time he's almost got it. Yes, it's in his mouth. There! Gee, folks, this is one of the most thrilling dinners I ever broadcast."

By this time Mickey and the Duke could plainly hear loud knocking and pounding from below. Someone was trying vehemently to force the lower door that led to the bell tower. "We hear someone below. Probably it's Colonel Apted of the Harvard Mounties who always gets his man. If we are able to persuade him, folks, we'll try to get him to come before the mike as our guest speaker here tonight. Next week at the same time we hope to have that distinguished alumnus of Yale, Rudy Vallée. What's that? Word has just reached me from the Fly Club that each new member has to give a sort of skit during the evening, and as the President's son is being initiated, he will distinguish himself with a special dance. Looks like this would be some dance, folks, some dance. Apted's water-pistol Mounties are going to like this dance apparently. I can see a couple of them on guard in the dining room drawing their guns. One man has a wicked-looking six-shooter. I'd sure hate to run into one of those boys on a dark night.

"No. Oh, no, Mr. President. Not that fork. Not that one for peas, Mr. President. Remember the eyes of the nation, the whole world, are upon you at the moment. Two forks to the right. The second to the right. That's the one. That's the pea fork. Whew! He almost made a bad mistake. That was a tough moment, folks, the President nearly chose the wrong fork to go to work on his peas. Now the music is starting. The President's son is starting to dance. Ladies and gentlemen, I wish you could be here to look down as we do and see the remarkable footwork of this fine specimen of clean young American manhood. Six feet three, if he's an inch. Such grace, such agility. Now he's on his ear. His left ear, I think, but it's hard to tell exactly. He's caught hold of the table. It's tipping over. There it goes . . . there it . . . no, the President caught it just in time. Just . . ." For the first time his smooth running fire of conversation hesitated. Mickey rushed breathlessly into the room and banging the door, locked it. Fog quickly collected himself.

"That noise you heard, folks, was Colonel

Apted's water-pistol. The trusty head of the Harvard Mounties is hard on the trail of some scoundrel, I doubt not. Maybe we can persuade him to pause in his fight against crime long enough to say a few words to the radio audience. Ah . . . I hear him now. We'll pause a moment for station announcement."

Mickey stepped to the amplifier. "This is Station L-O-W-E-L-L folks, and the Dunster Funsters bringing you a plate-by-plate broadcast description of the hundredth anniversary dinner of the Fly Club, attended by the President of the United States. Now I'll turn the microphone back to Ted Hooey. Take it away, Ted."

"Thank you, Graham."

"And thank you, Ted."

"No, Graham, I thanked you first." By this time the door was bending, notwithstanding the efforts of the Duke to hold it in place from the assaults of three men outside. Over the uproar and shouts, above the noise of the splintering door, Fog's voice came clearly.

"Yes, it's the Colonel himself. I can't see him, but I can see his big .45 caliber water-pistol through a crack in the door. My, what a sight to make a man's blood freeze in his veins. Maybe we can persuade the Colonel to say just a few words. Come right in, Colonel. Bring your men with you. And don't forget your pistol. Folks, it gives me great pleasure to—great pleasure to introduce—"

There was a commotion in the tower. A crash. Then without ceremony the broadcast ended. Cheers and shouts of "More" "More," came from the street. But the Dunster Funsters had signed off for the evening. And forever.

11

C ome in," said the Duke, alone in the room.
The door opened and a man with a ruddy
face and graying hair stood there.

"Mr. Wellington?"

"Sorry, I have a pressing contract."

"I just dropped in . . ."

"The Coop. does our laundry. I never . . ."

"No, I came round to see whether . . ."

But the Duke had watched Mickey and Fog
dispose of canvassers for some months now, and
he was an expert at the job.

"Don't subscribe for any magazines, and my roommate is the one who buys all the books."

"Wait a minute. I'm Ned Ellis, the track coach."

Of course. Ellis, the track coach. That was where he'd seen him before, on Soldier's Field. He felt ashamed of his technique now.

"I'm terribly sorry. We get such a lot of people here trying to sell us something, my roommates have taught me to be pretty hardboiled. Sit down, won't you? I used to see you on Soldier's Field last year when I was playing football."

The visitor was surprised and showed it in his voice. "Football! Did you play on the freshman? You don't look heavy enough for football."

"No. I'm not heavy enough. Or good enough, either. I played some at home in high school, but there was too much competition here in Cambridge. I didn't even last the season on the squad, got dropped on the final cut."

"No wonder. That was a heavy team, that freshman team last year. You must have taken a good deal of punishment. What'd you play, end?"

"I tried to."

"Play anything else in high school?"

"Yes, basketball."

"D'je ever run?"

"No. Never, that is until last month."

"That was a crazy thing to do. You might have ruined yourself. How did you manage to do it? And how did you stand it afterward?"

"I felt pretty bad the next few days, I'll admit. The calves of my legs are only just coming round now. They were so stiff I could hardly walk for a week . . . like boards they were."

"Yes, I can understand that. I was up there at the finish when you came in. Never expected you to pull it off. You say you never ran before at all?"

"No. And just now I feel I never want to run again." The coach responded with a laugh, a hearty laugh. He was different from the football coaches, more human and approachable. "Yes, you feel like that right now, I can appreciate. Do you smoke much?"

"No, not at all." What was he getting at?

"Drink?"

"Nope."

"Ever consider coming out for track?"

"Why no, I never did." So that was it. "The one taste I had of running was just about enough to last me all through college."

"You did a very foolish thing. Let's see, your

roommate is McGuire, the varsity quarterback, isn't he?"

"One of them. He's out tonight, but he'll be back soon."

"I'd like to see him. But I came round to look you up. Anyone that can walk twelve miles, let alone run twelve miles, ought to be out for track. Most of you fellows have lost the use of your legs nowadays. Automobiles. Pretty soon there won't be any legs left in America. But McGuire knows something about sport, he shouldn't ever have let you try such a thing without training. Now see here, you're material for the cross-country squad and the track team. I'd like to see you come out."

The Duke was pleased and warmed by his personality. But the thought of going through all the business of training, of registering, of making the effort only to be dropped again from another squad, was frightening. He shook his head.

"Don't think I can spare the time. You see I got off to a bad start and was on pro at the November Hours. That was because I spent my afternoons playing football and was too tired to work much nights. Had to devote the rest of the year, every minute, to making up . . ."

"But running doesn't take much time. Besides, they tell me you are almost on the Dean's list."

This man knew everything! Even the Duke himself wasn't sure where he stood. He realized the effort he had made was beginning to count, that he was now able to work faster and get more things done, that his classes were easier. But he'd told no one of his ambition to make the Dean's list, nor that his marks were gradually rising.

"Well, you see my dad expects things. He's made a big sacrifice to send me East to college and I sort of want to make good if I can."

"Looks to me like you will. But you have to get some exercise sometimes, don't you?"

"I play squash."

"Well, why not give us a try for a couple of weeks. It won't take any more time than squash. Come down and see how you like running. I think you'd enjoy it and you might do well. Except for Whitney we haven't any good varsity material for the distances now. Just come once and try it, won't you?" He was persuasive and hard to refuse. The Duke, however, tried.

"I haven't any outfit. And I'm not buying anything just now, overdrawn my allowance."

"We're running on the boards. We'll fix you up with short spikes. Come down tomorrow and see how you like it, that's all I ask."

The Duke promised. When he got down to the Locker Building that next afternoon, he wished at once that he hadn't. No one paid any attention to him. With difficulty he dug up a second assistant manager who gave him a running suit to cover his lanky frame, a pair of short-spiked running shoes, and socks. It was cold on the board track, a bitter wind was blowing across from the ice-covered river. Only the coach seemed to know what he was to do.

"Hullo there, Wellington, glad to see you out. Take a couple of laps with these men, will you?" Without more ceremony he fell in with a group of men led by some varsity runner with an H on his track suit, and loped half a dozen times round the hard track. It was not fun. They stopped.

"Dick. C'm over here." The coach called to the man with the H who came across to the Duke. "This is Wellington, remember? Man I was speaking to you about yesterday. This is Whitney, cross-country captain."

"Glad to see you."

"Glad to meet you. Heard about your stunt

last month. Say, that was some trek. Ever run before?"

"Nope. Never did."

"You'll like it. Lots of fun."

But the Duke decided it wasn't his idea of fun at all. He reported regularly for ten days, each colder than the one before. Snow fell and was shoveled off the track so they could run. Winds smacked them as they came up one side. The coach stood round, his hands in the pockets of his ulster and his ears red, shivering. On the whole he found it took as much time as football, and there was no fun or variety in it. Slug, slug, and slug round that monotonous track. He had about decided to quit when he arrived one afternoon at the lockers to hear a mystic phrase being passed about. Time trials.

An hour later he was standing halfway round the icy track. Just across from him was Whitney standing by the coach with his pistol upraised. In between were numerous runners scattered at various marks and he observed that he had been given the largest handicap of them all. Almost a hundred and fifty yards. The voice of the coach, unusually sharp and authoritative, came through the wind.

"Now then. Now then, you men. Ready! Get set." And the pistol barked. The Duke's heart beat as the boards trembled with the stamping feet. He realized he was in a race. Clumsily and with effort he started away from the gaining pack behind.

It really wasn't much of a race. A hundred and fifty yards in eight hundred is a good deal as he was to realize later, and it didn't take much to keep ahead of those pounding feet in the rear. The Duke had no technique, no knowledge of running, no sense of timing or pace, nothing but long legs and an ability to take punishment. It was as simple as that. He was far ahead at the start and, to his elation, ahead when he came up to the last bank. He put everything he had into a spurt, not daring to look back at the pursuers behind. The coach stood there, watch in hand, while they finished.

"All right, you men. Don't stand out here in the cold. Get right in and have a rubdown. Whitney, come here a minute." The Duke, sitting with his head between his legs on the top bank of the first turn, watched the coach and the captain as he got stiffly up. They were looking first at the watch and then over at him. The time must have been all right.

He went inside, had a shower and dressed slowly. Maybe this wasn't such a bad sport after all. Maybe there was more in it, yes, there was more in it than you'd ever imagine. Maybe he'd make a runner out of himself. Why not? He glanced up and saw the coach standing over him as he sat on the bench before his locker. The coach's ears were red and so was his nose.

"Don't report tomorrow, Wellington. Nor Friday. I may use you in the 880-yard relay against Holy Cross in the B.A.A. Games on Saturday. Just take it easy the next two days."

The Duke carefully neglected to tell either of his roommates he was running. He'd tell them tonight when he got back. No, tell them at dinner. No, let them read it in the *Crimson* on Saturday. He could see Mickey, disheveled, in his bathrobe, picking up the *Crimson* from under the door and reading the notice.

". . . against Holy Cross in the 880-yard relay, James H. Wellington, Jr. . . ."

Make the track team! Yes, sir, he might get his H after all. Gosh, wouldn't that make Dad proud. He'd forget about the football. That would probably mean one of the clubs, too. It would mean everything—everything Father had wanted for him. His legs were as stiff as they had been that day after the big race, but he almost ran across the bridge and down beside the river. How could he ever keep from telling them, anyway? Fog would guess something was up. He laughed at the thought of the broadcast and Fog, the perfect announcer. What a stir that had made. For a week they'd been pretty nervous, all of them.

He came into the entry and up the stairs. It hurt to go up the steps, but he didn't mind. The room was alight and he pushed open the door. Both of them were inside, alone and for once silent. They saw him.

"Shall we tell the worst, Mickey?"

"You tell him, big boy. It was all your idea."

"Yes, I suppose it was—Duke, I regret to report . . ." He looked at a card in his hand and extended it. "I regret to report that the Dunster Funsters, each and every one, are on probation. . . . Or soon will be."

"W-what?" It wasn't possible. He looked down at the card. "You are requested to report at the office of the Dean at University 4 between 10-12 on Friday, February 20." There were two more cards on the table.

12

The Duke stepped out of the car at Albany to get some air. A man in his class was hurrying across the platform evidently to join the train. Now the Duke had no such thing as class spirit; he decided he even lacked that fetish of most universities, college spirit. Nevertheless, he was glad to see this friendly face in the crowd. They sat in the Pullman together talking and watching the sweep of the Berkshires as they passed, all red and gold, before them, and while they talked it began to dawn upon him that at last he really belonged. At last he was a part, an insignificant part but a unit, in the enormous and amazing place that was Harvard. For the first time in three years he was coming into Cambridge without loneliness and dread in his heart. He belonged, and that was a lot more than some of those stuffed-shirted individuals did. The war was over. He was on his feet. There were problems ahead; for one thing he was still on probation with his roommates, but anyhow things were better and a load was lifted from his mind.

At seven they went into the diner, joking with each other because on the menu was that awful roast beef au jus that was served every other night at Dunster House. He hadn't seen it or thought of roast beef au jus all summer. This didn't bother him, however, nor did Pierson, the senior who joined them toward the end of the meal and spent half an hour telling what a wonderful time he had had on his estate in a way that once would have angered the Duke. One got used to everything. Now it merely amused him.

Fog was in the middle of their room the next morning when he reached Dunster House. This was a new Fog, tanned, weather-tough, with little lines at the corners of his eyes caused by winds off the ocean. He had spent his whole vacation sailing a thirty-foot sloop to Bermuda and back with two companions. It had aged him, given him an older look, but otherwise he was the same Fog with the same way of looking at you in a questioning manner so that unless you knew him pretty well you were never quite sure whether he was kidding or not.

"And Mickey? When does Mickey get here? This afternoon?" Registration was the next morning.

Entirely surrounded by huge leather bags which he was unpacking in the simplest method—throwing the contents in a heap on the couch and the bags in a big closet, Fog glanced up. "The McGuire, let me hasten to inform you, has been here since the fifteenth. Tough as board, too. He's been working as some sort of a lumberman up in the northwest. Have you forgotten that your roommate is one of the illustrious great of this institution, and a pillar of fire on the football eleven?"

"Oh! Then we're off pro!" Like Fog he had treated it all more or less as a joke. His marks were good enough to make him excitingly near the Dean's list, and he was not worried, especially as he had managed to convert his father to Fog's jocular attitude toward the whole proceeding. Of course there had been drawbacks. No running, for instance. Just when he had got off to a good start, too. And then no cuts at classes. Yes, it had all been very funny, but there were disadvantages about being on probation. Another load fell away from him.

It was quickly replaced.

"Not at all. Who said we were off. We aren't off pro. Yet."

"Well . . . I mean . . . but how can Mickey play football then? I thought no one on probation could take part in any organized . . ."

"My dear Duke." The bags were unpacked so Fog sat down in an empty chair and lit a cigarette. "Surely by this time you know how things work in this great university? Do you suppose the Dean's Office doesn't know that every good player on the squad is given a free ticket to Wolf's Tutoring School, so they can make up lost work after the season is over? Of course they do. But they just ignore it. So they ignore Mickey's presence on Soldier's Field. Know it? Naturally they know it. But officially he isn't there. That's the whole purpose of being a Dean, to be able to ignore things you don't wish to know about. They are international champion ignorers. Except when they find themselves pushed into a corner as we pushed them publicly by that broadcast. Then they have to take steps. Alas! Mickey probably won't get into the Amherst game next Saturday. Do you imagine that will affect our chances? You think not? I agree. But suppose he doesn't play against Dartmouth two weeks later, or Army the week after that. Ah, there now. . . ."

"I see."

"Marvelous. After two years here it's about time. The H.A.A. moves in devious ways its wonders to perform. The only varsity quarterback is McGuire. The only quarterback in college who can be trusted not to stall the team on the eight-yard line is McGuire. The only kicker, the only open-field runner, the only passer and all-round player on the squad is your roommate, the lazy, likable, the mighty McGuire."

"So you mean they'll take him off pro to play football?"

"Certainly not. We don't do things that way

at Harvard. We never put it bluntly as you middle-westerners always insist on doing. I mean that he is off probation now. Unofficially. Those paladins, the football coaches, have means of access to the college records which are hidden to mortals like ourselves."

"Then he'll be taken off soon? Is that it? And what about us?"

"He will. And we will. Unfortunately, or rather fortunately from our point of view, you cannot separate the Dunster Funsters. One for all and all for one. That's the motto of the university, isn't it . . . it isn't? No, of course not. It's the motto of the United States. Or maybe of Rotary International. Anyhow, they can't save McGuire for touchdowns without saving Smith, the man who caused all the trouble at the Fly Club dinner, and Wellington, the radio mechanic who aided and abetted. I trust, Duke, that this episode did not penetrate the hinterlands of your native heath. . . ."

"You mean you hope it got out that far. Rest assured. It did. Even the Indians on the prairie are talking about you, Foggie."

"Really. And I suppose the moment you return to a normal undergraduate status and the ban is lifted, that you will push off once more for the track on Soldier's Field? Thus adding to the athletic renown of Dunster H 35?"

"Maybe. I haven't yet made up my mind."

"Ah. What seems to be the trouble?"

"Nothing, except that I'm more interested in making the Dean's List than in making the track team. If I can make either."

"It seems to me you could make both as you practically did last spring. It's been done before this, you know."

"I know it has. Isn't such a tremendous feat. But it is for me. That football tryout my freshman year taught me a lesson. Least I hope it did. You remember how I was. Couldn't study and play ball, so my work suffered. Then I'm no darn good at all in examinations; they get me down, Fog. The moment I go into an exam I go to pieces. So I have to study harder during the year to make up for them. If it was a question of being on the Dean's List or a second-rate man on the track team, I don't think I'd hesitate. But what about you, Fog? Have a good time this summer? And how is the *Lampoon* coming along?" Fog's famous broadcast had put him and his room-mates on probation, but it had also won him a place on the editorial board of the *Lampoon,* the college comic magazine.

"Lampy's doing first rate, thanks. I have an idea or two . . ."

Thumps and bumps on the stairs. A heavy step on the entry floor below. A shout.

"Hey, you guys." The door flew open and there he stood as usual, that Irish grin on his face. "And there's the Duke himself."

Yes, it was good, it was awfully good to be back. For the first time he was happy to be in this place where no one ever called him Jim.

13

Two years previously, even a year earlier, the Duke would hardly have known how to handle such a situation. But he had been living two long winters with Mickey and Fog and had learned a thing or two. So he was impervious to the polite hints of the older man that he was the person they had come to see.

"These gentlemen are my close friends. You can speak right out in front of them. Say anything you like."

There was Ellis, the track coach, gray-haired and smiling; there was Whitney, lean and sinewy and unloquacious; and the third visitor was Thurber, the captain, an intercollegiate champion shot-putter and also a varsity tackle. Sitting on the edge of those stiff wooden chairs they looked uncomfortable. McGuire was the only really unconcerned person in the room because Fog was a close friend of Thurber's and knew beforehand that this committee was visiting the Duke. He had hoped to be out when they called.

Mickey stuck his hands behind his head. Maybe this would be fun. "What seems to be the trouble, Ned?" McGuire had hardly seen the track coach before, but he invariably called everyone by his first name. It was part of his charm because he did it in such an ingenuous way that strangers were warmed and attracted to him. The coach smiled.

"We've come up here to put the heat on your roommate, McGuire." Anyone could call a track coach by his first name, but calling a varsity quarterback by his first name was another matter.

"You see, Wellington, the situation is like

this." The captain turned toward the Duke. He had a private school accent and was a Bostonian of the Bostonians. As he leaned earnestly forward, the Duke counted the number of times he had been introduced to this man since coming to college. First at the freshman smoker. Then at the Union the night of that political rally. Next in the bar of the Ritz the night he went in to pick up Fog when they were going to a show together. Oh, yes, and during the dance at the Brattle Hall when Thurber was an usher. There must have been at least a couple more meetings, but the Duke couldn't recall them. Each time Thurber had stuck out his hand and said, "How do you do, Mr. Wellington." And the Duke had stuck out his hand and said, "How do you do, Mr. Thurber." Gravely, as if they had never met before. And the next morning in History 12, they hadn't spoken. Well, that was Cambridge.

This was Cambridge, too, this group here. Mickey grinning, trouble in his Irish eyes, scenting a fight somewhere and anxious to see it happen, Fog well groomed and ironical in his armchair, Thurber slightly embarrassed because he had to ask favors of someone he didn't really like, and the coach quiet and persuasive, watching his job nailed down if the Duke ran and helped win. For there was a good chance to capture the Intercollegiates. "For the first time since 1909," explained Thurber, his accent jabbing the Duke with every word. The coach, wise and understanding, read this in his face and interrupted the captain.

"You see, Wellington, it comes down to this. We have plenty of material to beat Dartmouth. I think we can beat Yale, and Yale is the strongest team in the East this year. We have Thurber in the weights and jumps, Whitney in the mile or half, Foster in the dashes and Everard in the hurdles. That's a team of world-beaters. We need one more good point winner. If you ran the two-mile I could possibly use Whitney in the half. Your points might make all the difference."

The Duke was polite but unresponsive. "I'm afraid I'm no world-beater."

"That's what we don't know yet."

"Maybe so, but——"

"You haven't had a time trial. How do you know what you can do?" said the coach, Whitney, and Thurber all together. They spoke in unison and stopped in unison. There was silence.

"You have to get exercise every day, don't you, Wellington?" asked Thurber.

"It takes no more time than squash," added the coach. Mickey saw a look come into his roommate's eyes. This was going to be fun.

"Well . . . it's like this. I don't just know why you fellows came to Harvard. I don't know why you came here, Thurber, but I know why I came. My father pushed me here." There was an embarrassed laugh from Thurber and a little chuckle from Mickey. He was right. This was going to be good.

"It's a funny place, Harvard. But it does give you one thing. A sense of values." He glanced about the room. Mickey's face was eager with interest. Fog was watching him intently. They had never heard the Duke like this before. He hadn't heard himself, either. "Yep, it gives you a sense of values. What for do I want to waste my time plugging round that track when I can get something much better—"

"But your exercise, man. You can't study all the time. You've got to exercise once in a while."

The Duke turned on him. "Thurber, that's the old timeworn saw I first heard freshman year. I used to fall for it then. Suppose I'll hear it just as long as I'm in Cambridge. Once I believed that. I went down and gave everything I had for football. At night I was good for nothing. Too tired even to hold my head up. The result was probation and one year of hell."

"But look here. You're nowhere near probation now. Your marks are almost good enough to put you on the Dean's List."

"Thurber, let me tell you something. Out home where I come from most of the boys go from High School to State in Iowa City. I came East to Harvard. Do you happen to know the difference between Harvard and State?"

"In money? Why, no, couple of hundred bucks?"

"About a couple of thousand. That's all. Tuition there is $60, and here it's $400. Everything else in scale. My dad isn't rich—he drives a Ford. Made all sorts of sacrifices to get me here and keep me here. So I'm going to climb on that Dean's List or bust. That's why I won't bother with your team, even if I liked you or your crowd. Which I don't."

The coach rose. He saw the two were getting nowhere. "Think it over, Wellington. We need you. You'd get lots of fun out of running and I believe you'd enjoy it. Maybe you'll change your mind."

The Duke recalled those cold, raw afternoons on the windswept board track, and was sure he wouldn't like it. Nor did he think as the group broke up that he was likely ever to change his mind. The track men passed out of the door, and he saw them passing from his life.

Which was full enough without them. That fall passed quickly. It hardly seemed a week from that evening at the start of college to the cold, sunswept afternoon in the Yale Bowl when he watched Mickey down on the field, supremely efficient, sure of himself as he'd been that day as a freshman. Yes, Mickey was just the same. That gesture of holding the ball out to a tackler and then taking it away again, that cool way in which he waited until the last second and then dived into a hole in the line, coming up in the Yale backfield, edging off to one side, shaking off a lunging body or darting suddenly away from the pack. Even his figure was the same: stocky, decisive, and trim. Mickey hadn't changed, but the Duke felt a thousand years older than the day he had watched the then unfamiliar figure run through the freshmen on Soldier's Field.

It was fall, then Thanksgiving, then all at once it was early winter. That sudden passage of time was mostly because of his work. He had made the exciting discovery that his work was stimulating. Occasionally vistas of great horizons were opened up by his instructors, especially Salvemini, an old Italian with fire and vitality, and by Hawkins, a sharp, incisive and homely little man who taught literature. He found himself aroused and inspired. His work had in it none of the drudgery of his freshman year, and for the first time the examinations at Midyears were an amusing hurdle to meet, an interlude and not a horrible test which worried him day and night. They came, and they also passed, like the Yale game, and the Christmas vacation which again he spent in the House Library.

The first snowfall of the year was at the beginning of February. The Duke walked down from the Square late one afternoon in a thick snowstorm. He speculated on its probable length, wondered whether he could induce Mickey and Fog to go on a snow-train over the weekend. Midyears were finished. A vacation was in order. Yes, Midyears were finished and yet his marks weren't out. Funny that, because both his roommates had theirs. He stumbled into the lighted entry, shaking off the snow, and went upstairs. Mickey, on his knees, was stirring a log in the fireplace.

"Cold in this room. We need some more wood. By the way, Duke, there's a note there from the Office for you."

Sure enough, there was an envelope on the table. Not the familiar card shoved under the door, but a regular envelope addressed to him from the Office of the Dean. There was a two-line note inside.

The Duke's head went round. "HEY! Mickey! Look!" He held out the note and reached for the telephone.

Mickey read it. "Nice work, kid. Well, we all knew you could do it. And—to think I was tutoring you freshman year! Remember—three E's, a C, and a D, and now four B's or more."

"Gimme Western Union," said the Duke. "Western Union? Wanna send a wire to Waterloo, Iowa. W-A-T-E-R-L-O-O . . ."

Mickey slipped out the door and went down for the wood. The outer door opened as he reached the bottom landing, and in came Ellis, the track coach, followed by a whirl of snow.

"Hi, Ned," said McGuire.

"Oh . . . hullo, McGuire. Your roommate in now?"

"Yep. Right upstairs. And . . . I think you can sell him a bill of goods, too. He's just made the Dean's List."

14

Mickey rarely exercised his wit at the expense of his two roommates, but the winter was long, the weather endlessly dismal, and things in February were boring. That evening he sat with his feet on the desk, thumbing over the pages of the last *Lampoon*.

"How much do we pay for this rag, Duke?"

The Duke at his desk was working. He hardly paid attention.

"Four bucks, isn't it?"

"Four bucks! Holy codfish. That'll buy a good

seat at a Broadway show or the new text in Social Science everyone is supposed to read."

"I bought it," said the Duke tersely.

"Oh. You did, did you? Well, anyway, four bucks is four bucks. Now if we didn't have your esteemed roommate to think about—"

"What do you want for your money, Mickey, the earth?" Fog tossed aside the *Transcript* and roused himself to defend the *Lampoon*. "What's the matter with it?"

"Matter! S'no good. No darn good at all. I can't get a laugh in a carload of those *Lampoons* of yours. And the drawings. High school stuff." The feeling came to him that he was going to annoy Fog and his mischievous spirit was afire to see whether his roommate would rise to the bait. "By the way, just what is your job on that rag, Foggie?"

Fog refused to bite. He kept an air of indifference. "You wouldn't understand if I told you, Mickey. I'm an idea man. You don't know what ideas are. We live in a world of ideas. They surround us on every side. Yet if one came up on the street and spoke to you, you'd probably borrow a match and walk along. Every magazine has one man to furnish ideas, understand? Something original. Now—"

"You haven't been very busy lately, have you?"

The thrust registered, but Fog paid no attention. "Of course, naturally, sometimes one issue is better than another. I'll admit our February number is not up to our usual high standard—"

"Oh, you do, do you? That's pretty swell of you. But in the meantime, how about my four bucks? What do I get for my—"

"You mean your two bucks and the Duke's two bucks, I presume."

"Shut up, you guys. How can I study when you're jawing about the *Lampoon?*"

"I wasn't jawing. I was asking for information. Wondering what our big idea-man did to justify his name on the inside of the magazine, and what that tedious sheet would do without him. He never has any ideas around here—except to notice that there isn't any wood for the fireplace. Although he seldom lugs any upstairs himself."

"My ideas are valuable, Mickey. I can't afford to waste them on insensibles like you. As a matter of fact I'm off to a meeting of the Board this very minute. Just teeming with ideas, I am. You'll be surprised, my lad." And he hoisted himself out of the armchair and put on his coat.

"For the first time, then. No, I'm wrong. For

the first time since your infernal broadcast. I hope your ideas won't get the *Lampoon* into the mess you got Dunster H 35, Fog."

"In all probability my idea will make the *Lampoon* as celebrated throughout the nation as that broadcast made us famous in undergraduate circles, Mickey. Fact there's no telling how far it might carry."

"Okay, just so you don't start trouble with them as you did with a couple of innocent bystanders like the Duke and me. Better watch your step, kid."

Fog went down without any answer. The truth was that Mickey had managed to shake him. A good idea. Yes, that was what old Lampy needed. Needed badly, but what . . . how could he get one? He walked slowly up to the Square, bought another evening newspaper, went into the Georgian and ordered a cup of coffee. He opened the paper and read it. Same news as the earlier edition of the *Transcript*. Rearmament in Europe. Stocks off in Wall Street. Guesses in Boston as to the name of the new president of Harvard. The new president of Harvard. Wait a minute. He thought for a while. Then he got up. Yes, that was it. The new president. By George, that was an idea. Except for Mickey's prodding it might never have occurred to him, either.

Several days later Mickey spoke to the Duke about Fog. "Say, you know I believe that smart roommate of ours is up to some evil."

"Oh, yeah! What makes you think so?"

"Dunno. Just think so. For one thing he hasn't slept here for the last two nights. And I haven't seen him, either, for a couple of days. Have you?"

"Come to think of it, I haven't. Guess he's over at the *Lampoon*. About time for their next number, isn't it?"

"Yeah, but just the same he has something up his sleeve. Wait and see. I know that rascal. He was like this the week before the broadcast, remember? Whenever Fog is quiet this way, look out for trouble. Maybe he's planning another broadcast. Perhaps he's decided to rustle out that big idea we were kidding him about."

"You were kidding him, Mickey."

"All right. Have it your own way. What time is it? Seven? Let's go to a movie in town. To-morrow's a holiday, February 22, we can sleep late."

"So we can. Say, this is the night of the dance

at the *Lampoon* Building. That's where Fog is, of course, getting ready for the dance." So they put their things on and walked over to the subway. Back at eleven, they found Fog's clothes strewn about the bedroom, and evidently he had changed and gone to the dance. They sat round for an hour, and at midnight went to bed without any trace of Fog.

The Duke's voice was excited when he woke his roommate up at eight-thirty. "Get up, Mickey. That man Smith didn't come home again last night. His bed is untouched."

Mickey sat up, rubbing his eyes. With no classes, he had anticipated the luxury of a long, late sleep; and he was not happy at waking up. "Oh, what the dickens. What of it?" He yawned. "Never mind. He probably danced late and then got into a bender in the *Lampoon* Building. He'll roll up."

He got up and going into the bathroom started brushing his teeth when he heard the Duke from the study.

"What d'you think of that. C'm here." In the center of the room the Duke was reading the morning issue of the *Crimson*, and across the top of the paper in large black letters was the heading:

"CLARKE NEW HARVARD HEAD."

And underneath a picture of the man who had been chosen to be president of the University. For weeks and months the choice had been debated. At last it was announced.

"At a special meeting of the Board of Overseers, Henry Eliot Clarke, '04, of Evanston, Illinois, was chosen as the next president of Harvard University. The official announcement was made late last night. Mr. Clarke, though comparatively little known in the East, has long been prominent in middle-western educational circles, especially since his appointment to the Board of Trustees of Chicago University in 1925." Then came a column of descriptive matter. Adjoining it was another column.

"Business and educational interests have gone side by side in the career of Henry Eliot Clarke, '04, the new president of Harvard. He was born in Davenport, Iowa, January 16, 1887, the son of William and Elizabeth (Eliot) Clarke. In the fall of 1900 he matriculated at Harvard the same year as Franklin D. Roosevelt. As an undergraduate his career was rather inconspicuous. He was a good if not a brilliant student. He participated in several undergraduate sports but did not win a major H. He was also a member of the Areopagus Club, a group which disbanded about 1910."

After that followed a long account of his business career in the home office of Armour & Company, Chicago, his service during the war in an advisory capacity to the Inter-Allied Food Council, the positions of public service he had held, the directorates and clubs he belonged to. On another page was a telegram from his classmate, the president of the United States, a long one from the president of Columbia, and shorter ones from the presidents of Yale and Princeton. They were unanimous. He was the ideal man. It was to mark a new epoch in the history of Harvard.

The new president and his selection threw all thought of their wandering roommate from their minds. They dressed and went downstairs to breakfast. The morning *Herald* had a lengthy and complete story running much like that in the *Crimson*, save that it had no accompanying photograph. The New York papers on the other hand carried no mention of it. Inside the *Herald* was Mr. Clarke's wire of acceptance to the Board of Overseers.

"It is with profound surprise that I accept this

great office. For it is an office that carries with it a wonderful tradition of great men and great acts. It is indeed sobering to realize that I have been chosen to carry on this great tradition. Myself a graduate of Harvard, I love the Yard as only a graduate can, and I have tried to keep in close contact with it since graduation. My policies will be liberal, for such is the Harvard tradition and such is my own inclination as well. My two dearest beliefs are in individualism and democracy. My only hope is that I can soon adapt myself to the work and that I may be able to continue as far as possible in the spirit and with the skill that such a great office demands."

Clarke. A westerner. Born in Iowa, too! Harvard had turned for its president to the Middle West. It was a new era. You couldn't say the college was provincial anymore, could you? Fog was wrong when he declared that for most of the University the West began at Albany. The Duke attempted to point this out, but Mickey was silent. He was trying to figure where he had seen the man's face before.

"You know that face. . . . I've seen it somewhere. I can't tell where, but I know it." Just then Gordon Cross hurried past, leaned over, and spoke to one of the men at the table. He rushed on. "Hey, Gordon," called Mickey. "Where have I seen this man Clarke before?" Gordon was one of the editors of the *Crimson*. He would know.

But Gordon acted strangely. Instead of replying he looked at Mickey and went out of the room. "What is this?" said Mickey. "Wait a minute." And he went into the Common Room, returning in a minute with the issue of the day before's *Crimson*. He pointed to a small notice in one corner.

" 'Owing to the fact that tomorrow, February 22, is a holiday in all departments of the University, there will be no issue of the *Crimson*.' Now what do you make of that?"

"This issue today is an extra. See, stupid? An extra, get it, up there at the top. They had word late last night and came out with this extra." The rest of the table were satisfied but not Mickey. "Yeah, but all the same there's something phony. Did you read this, this stuff? 'Mr. Clarke is a great man, a man of vision, with stalwart strength, and with broad-minded enlightenment. A businessman, he is fitted to carry Harvard through, a middle-westerner he brings a new aspect which cannot help but be edifying, and finally, descendant of a New England family he bears a name famous in the annals of Harvard life. The *Crimson* feels awed by these qualifications and by his other great attributes. Mr. Clarke is a modern tycoon, one of the few American businessmen to weather the depression not with decay, but with an astounding fruition and development of his own labors. Now he returns to the University that nurtured him, and the *Crimson* feels awe at his coming, for we are essentially hero-worshipers. Aren't we all?' "

This rocked the table. For the first time there was doubt. Mickey shook his head. "Modern tycoon. I dunno about that one. Duke, come upstairs a minute." Once in their room, he picked up the telephone. "Commonwealth 2000. Hullo, *Herald?* Give me the managing editor. Well— whoever's in charge, then. Hullo. Say, can you give me any confirmation on the selection of that man Clarke for president of Harvard? You can't. You haven't. WHAT! He isn't . . . well . . . yes, I see . . . I thought maybe it was something like that. Thanks."

He turned to the Duke. "Well, your roommate, Mr. J. Faugeres Smith, is a honey, Duke.

That guy's good. Now let's see, what was it he said that night I was kidding him about his being an idea-man. You remember that night? Said his idea would make the *Lampoon* celebrated throughout the nation, didn't he? He's certainly made good."

The Duke was completely at sea. All he knew was that maybe something was wrong somewhere, and the man from Iowa wasn't president. "How do you mean? I don't get you. What has Fog got to do with the new president?"

"Everything. The managing editor of the *Herald* says there isn't any such man in the Harvard Alumni Directory as Henry Eliot Clarke of Chicago. Says all the Chicago newspapers have been carrying the story, and when they tried to check on the man, they couldn't locate him in Evanston, and he wasn't in *Who's Who*. That made 'em suspicious, so someone got an Alumni Catalogue, and when he wasn't there either they wired back here. There just isn't any such bird. It's Fog again."

"Fog again. I don't understand."

"Simple. That *Crimson* isn't a *Crimson*."

"You mean it's a fake *Crimson?*"

"Not a regular *Crimson*, anyway. Didn't you

notice the way Gordon Cross acted when I spoke to him at breakfast this morning? Somebody's pulled a fast one. There isn't supposed to be any *Crimson* today because it's a holiday. Just what I figured. So out comes this phony *Crimson* with the account of an election of a man named Henry Eliot Clarke. Swell name. Clarke, might be anything. Eliot, good old Harvard name. There just isn't any Henry Eliot Clarke with an E, and the new president hasn't been chosen. It's dirty work at the crossroads, and who would be up to such shenanigans except your roommate, the mighty Fog? Now the question is, how did he get it out? Who printed it? And what I'd like to know most of all, whose picture is it they used on the front page? I've seen that man somewhere before."

The door opened. There stood Fog. He was dirty, unshaven, tired, and red-eyed. He had been up all night; that was evident. His face was black and smudge-stained. His hands were grimy.

"Of course you've seen him, Mickey. He's the janitor of the *Lampoon* Building. Do I win now?"

"Win . . . you bet you win. . . ."

"But, Fog, how did you do it?"

"Was it your idea—who helped?"

They assailed him with questions. He sank into the armchair and lit a cigarette. "Well, it's like this. You sort of got under my skin, Mickey, with your jibes about my ideas, or lack of 'em. I had to pull out something to make good. Now what's been the one big topic of conversation around these parts since college opened?"

"The next president," said Mickey and the Duke together.

"Right. All we've been discussing since fall is the next president. An educator or a businessman? A professor or a go-getter? A New Yorker or a New Englander or a Middle Westerner? That's so, isn't it?" They both nodded assent. "So when I left the room that night, and bought an *Evening Globe,* it struck me in the eye that here was my issue. The *Globe* was full of rumors about several men who were possibilities, just as the *Transcript* had been. So the idea developed, and later at the Board meeting I put it up to the boys. It was Dick, I think, who remembered that the *Crimson* didn't publish on Washington's Birthday."

"You mean to say you did the whole thing in three days?"

"We did. Jim wrote that biography, wasn't it a honey? And Dick did Clarke's wire of acceptance and the telegrams from Butler and Seymour and a lot more of the stuff, and I wrote the editorial. I was rather proud of that editorial, you know, one of those long editorials full of words which don't mean anything—"

"Boy, you're good." For once Mickey was silent with admiration.

"I'm good, I admit, but Harry and Tom and Ned on the business staff are better. Know what they did? In the three days which was all we had, they canvassed the whole Square and saw every advertiser in the *Crimson*. Naturally they lined them all up, because they knew everyone would read a fake issue like this, so they gave us plates and we had exact copies of the *Crimson* ads. But the remarkable thing was that they stunned them into silence so that although the whole Square knew it, not a person on the *Crime* had a suspicion of what was coming."

"Yeah, those ads fooled me. They were the real thing. No question about it. . . ."

"Course they were the real thing. We had August and the Coop and Billings and Stover and Leavitts and Pinkos and the Georgian. And say—we even made money on the darn thing. A hundred and forty bucks!"

"Gosh." This impressed the Duke. To put one over on the *Crimson* was an achievement, to do it and show a profit on the venture was more so.

"But who distributed them?"

"That was a job. We've worked practically the whole time since Tuesday. None of us has been to classes for three days or had more than a couple of hours' sleep a night. Well, there was a dance at the *Lampoon* yesterday evening—"

"That's what threw me completely off," said Mickey. "I knew you were at the dance because we saw your clothes here in your room and knew you had put on evening clothes last night."

"Yeah, well, the dance broke up about three, and then we all changed our clothes and came back to work. There were six of us; let's see, Dick and Jim and I and Harry and Tom and Ned. We divided up the college—"

"Mean to say you distributed them yourselves?"

"Sure. I covered Winthrop, Dunster, Eliot, and McKinlock between three-thirty and six-thirty. Some job, let me tell you. By seven-thirty they were all out. But you see we had to slip them under the doors into the rooms, that took time."

"I noticed that," interrupted Mickey. "At least I thought the boys who bring round the *Crimson* were getting awful considerate. Usually they leave it out in the hall, but this one was in the room."

"Exactly. We had to slip them under the door because if they had been left in the hall, the editors of *Crimson*, as soon as they got up, would have run round and grabbed them all away. Believe me, that was a job. On top of three solid days' work. My back is broken. Then came the fun. Naturally there wasn't anyone in the *Crimson* office, so I went round and got in through a back window. Then Jim called up the Boston papers from our office, and said he was Professor Simpkins and what did they know about Mr. Clarke, the new president? They nearly fainted. That's how they got it. Instantly, of course, the phone in the *Crimson* office started ringing. So I answered, and said yes, this was the *Crimson*, that the college had given us a scoop, and that now it was out they were welcome to run the story themselves—"

"Did they fall?"

"Did they fall? Well, you saw the *Herald*. I believe the A.P.—they called up, too—carried it over their whole wire service, about a hundred and thirty papers all over the country. In twenty minutes that place was a maze of long distance calls from the Chicago *Daily News* and the *New York Times* and all over."

"And that's the janitor of the *Lampoon* building, is it? I knew I'd seen him somewhere before."

"Certainly. We simply put a wing collar and a striped tie on him, took his picture, and then reproduced it dully like the lousy cuts in the *Crimson*. Well, I'm going to take a shower and go to bed." He rose and peeled off his coat. The Duke was stunned. His feeling veered from admiration for the audacity of his roommate to disappointment that a son of Iowa was not to lead the college.

"Only one thing I don't understand, Mickey." Fog paused on the threshold of his bedroom. "How did you ever get the idea it was phony? We thought we had the thing foolproof. Ads, editorial, athletic notices, why, we even had a letter to the editor. Jim figured it would rock the boys on the *Crime* for a minute. How'd you get on to us, smarty?"

Mickey grinned. "Your weather report, boy. That was a giveaway." He picked up the copy of the fake *Crimson* from the desk. In the lower right hand corner was the weather forecast.

"Forecast for Cambridge. Storm brewing."

15

He rose, threw off the bedclothes, and opened the bedroom door. What he saw made him think he was dreaming. Just as he had once imagined, there stood Mickey in his tattered bathrobe reaching down to pick up the *Crimson* from under the hall door, glancing at it, and calling to him.

"Yep. Here it is, Duke. You're down all right. See—" Through sleepy eyes the Duke read over his roommate's shoulder.

"Two miles. For Harvard: V. Barker. W. R. Whitney. J. H. Wellington, Jr. For Yale: F. C. Kennedy. H. B. Painton. K. Simpson."

"So they plan to run him in the two miles. Not so good for Whitney, is it? Aw, they enter 'em in every event, but they don't run in all of 'em." The Duke grabbed the sheet. His heart was beating and he was wide awake now. Well, whether Painton ran or not, he had an H.A.A. They couldn't take that away from him. And if Painton didn't run—at least he had a chance for his H.

The day dragged. How the day dragged. The Duke went to a couple of classes in which every minute was an hour. It was the longest day he ever lived. Never had the time between eight and four seemed so eternal. Never before had time stood still like that. He got hot and cold, nervous and relaxed in turn. What was the use of worrying, he kept saying to himself, and five minutes later he was speculating on the chances of Painton running the two mile. After all, what did it matter? Only a race, wasn't it? No, it wasn't. It was a lot more than a race—if he did well. It was the Circle. Father had belonged to the Circle. Father expected him to. Father would understand his not making the Circle as a no-body, but as a member of the track team, that was different. Times had changed, things were different now, but how could you explain all that to Father?

The training table in the Varsity Club was an ordeal. No one could eat lunch; some drank milk and gulped a little food. Everyone talked in monosyllables except when Painton's name was mentioned, and apparently he was competing in every event. Afterward, a man tried to play the piano. "Aw, for Pete's sake, stop that noise," shouted half a dozen voices. The Duke drifted back to his room. There was a telegram on the table. It said simply, "Good luck. Father."

He tried to lie down and sleep. All he could see was the newspaper pictures of Painton; Painton winning the two mile in the last Intercollegiates, Painton winning the cross-country championships, Painton beating someone to the tape in a desperate struggle. If only he would stick to the mile. Why shouldn't a man be content with one race? He tried to read but couldn't. Then Mickey bumped into the room and flung open his door. Mickey knew. "Why, sure, kid, we all go through this." He sat down on the bed and stroked his legs. "We all get this way before every game. Worse than football? No, just the same. Don't worry, when you're like this it means you'll run well once you get out there. Wait and see. I'm an old-timer at this business. You'll come out up front—no matter who wins."

They walked down to the field together, Mickey encouraging, reassuring him. Painton probably wouldn't run the two mile, he had a tough enough time in the mile. As they reached the gates a pistol shot sounded from the stadium, and a roar came across to them. The roar grew to a crescendo and then died away. "Sounds pretty good for Harvard," said Mickey as they came inside the gate. Together they paused on the steps of the Locker Building listening to the loud-speaker.

"440-yard run. Won by—" Then a pause. "K. D. Sampson, Hahvud." The cheers broke out. "Second. J. Poole, Jr., Yay-ull. Third, S. B. Davis, Yay-ull. Time; forty-nine seconds."

"Hey, Mickey, what about that? Sampson beat Poole."

"He was expected to. Did you notice Yale won the other two places? That's where they'll clean up, seconds and thirds." They waited to watch the runners from the stadium who had just finished come into the lockers. Funny what a difference victory means in your after-race attitude. It was easy to tell the winner from those who hadn't placed. He came along panting but smiling, walking easily and quickly, answering the congratulations of the men who passed. Behind were two Harvard men who had failed to place. They hobbled as they walked, and one stopped, leaned over, retched and vomited. Ten yards further along the other man did the same thing.

"C'mon, Duke. You better dress." They went in and up the stairs. Men in track suits were coming down. The locker room was crowded. The Duke took his clothes out and dressed slowly. He began to wonder whether he might simulate sickness so he wouldn't have to run, and then whether he wouldn't actually be sick and be unable to run. He heard them talking about Painton. Covered up with a blanket and crouched in a corner, he heard them tell how Painton had won the mile. "His sprint was like nothing you ever saw. He just came after Dick as if he was on wheels." That was good news. If Painton ran the mile, he probably wouldn't run two miles. Suddenly the death sentence was announced.

"First call for the two-mile. All two-milers outside, please."

He rose, treading the pockmarked stairs gingerly in his stocking feet. His long-spiked shoes were in his hand, and on the steps outside he put them on and tied them carefully. There was another burst of cheering from the stadium, runners were coming in slowly, exchanging bits of news with the men going out. "Pole is at twelve-two." "Yale won the broad jump." "Four Harvard men in the finals of the two-twenty." "About even—guess it all depends on the two-mile, George."

That was it. Painton would surely run then. He walked over to the protecting wall of the stadium, and crept up inside its shelter, hidden from above. In a minute he was at the starting point where the Clerk of the Course with his board and paper was checking off the names of the starters.

"Barker."

"Here."

"Whitney."

"Here."

"Wellington."

"Here." His voice was cracked and dry. Whitney noticed it and looked over quickly with a smile. "Stay right with me, big boy," he whispered.

"Kennedy."

"Here."

"Painton."

"Here."

So that was the famous Painton. Yes, he was running all right, he was to win the meet for Yale. The Duke looked at him curiously. The familiar face and figure he had seen so often on the sports pages, the celebrated Painton of Yale. He wore a blue sweater with an enormous white Y on it, which he was removing. He tossed the sweater aside, and smoothed down his blond hair parted in the middle. You would never know he had just run a mile in fast time; he looked fresh and keen as he jumped up and down elastically. Then he saw Whitney, leaned over, and shook hands. Nervous? No, there was the same competent air and confident manner Mickey had on the gridiron. This man was going places and knew it. Well, that meant the meet for Yale and no H for the Duke. They couldn't expect Whitney to beat him, even in his second race of the day. The Duke felt glad the responsibility wasn't his. Mechanically he took his place, heard the starter advising them not to beat the gun, not to cut in on the turns. He crouched half down. He'd do his—

And the gun went off.

It left him standing still. Despite all the coach's instructions, too. They were five yards ahead when he gathered himself, furious at his mistake, and rushed after the bunch, forgetting his form, forgetting everything he had been told.

Afterwards he couldn't remember much about that race except pain. Pain and the cinders from the men ahead which cut into his legs as he ran. It was nine minutes of steady pain, for the pace was fast. Inexperienced as he was, he knew that. Somewhere about the fourth or fifth lap by desperate running he managed to get up behind Whitney. Then he recalled noticing Whitney after a while fading away. Yes, actually dropping off until only that cursed blue figure remained ahead. Aching legs, tortured lungs, and an everlasting wrangle with that blue jersey on a curve. Arms up, elbows, elbows.

Suddenly he saw eager faces grouped about the finish. They were shouting something, but in his agony he couldn't hear. It was all drowned in noise. Then the tape flicked on his chest, and he was stumbling, falling, and lying in agony on the grass.

In a minute Mickey was trying to embrace him. "I knew you could do it, kid. I knew you had it in you."

For a long time he couldn't get up. His legs were iron rods that pained him every step he took. Someone handed him a track suit. He started to climb into it, slipped, and would have fallen if Mickey hadn't caught his elbow. Supported by his roommate he hobbled across the field. There was a ripple of noise as he came to the end of the stands, and even in his pain and exhaustion he could distinguish voices of his classmates and friends above.

"Great work, Duke." "Attaboy, Duke." "Hey, Duke, kid." Then the noise stopped. It was the loudspeaker again.

"Two mile." The silence was over the whole stadium, and from the baseball diamond behind came the crack of a bat and a ball. "Won by J. H. Wellington, Jr., Hahvud." A wave of cheering interrupted the announcer. "Second, H. B. Painton, Yay-ull. Third, W. R. Whitney, Hahvud. Time—" and he paused significantly, as everyone in the stands nodded to everyone else. It was fast. "Time," droned the announcer, "nine minutes, eighteen and one-fifth seconds."

A wild, impetuous gust of noise swept the reaches of the stadium. Mickey and the Duke were almost up to the Locker Building when the voice continued. "Making a new Hahvud-Yay-ull record."

————16————

The locker room also greeted him with delight, with especial delight, for he was theirs, one of them. Two hours, an hour before, he was an unknown junior, a man who had only been running a couple of months, the chap who roomed with McGuire, the varsity quarterback, celebrated only for that reason. Now he was a figure in his own right, a real person. They came up in twos and threes, awkwardly but sincerely to shake his hand. Did he know he'd beaten the college record by three seconds? Did he realize he'd won the meet? Thurber, most awkward of all, thanked him clumsily. The coach came through the room beaming. Yes, thought the Duke, that man Ellis was right and I was wrong. It is good fun to run. Darn good fun. When you win.

"Now then, Wellington, get right into the showers and I want Gus to go over you carefully. You needn't report Monday or Tuesday." He was looking ahead to the Intercollegiates in two weeks' time. So the Duke found himself being undressed. Someone was pulling off his sweaty running shoes, and he was in the warm, welcoming shower. Finally out to the rubbing tables. Everyone was talking and calling to him. The whole place was relaxed and excited and noisy now, the tense atmosphere of the afternoon had vanished. Even Gus, the big rubber, was exhilarated.

"You bane do prutty good, Meester Wellington, yah. I say you prutty good runner fust time I see you."

Then dressing slowly, and the walk up to the House. Mickey was waiting for him down outside in the late afternoon sunlight. Made the Duke think of that time his freshman year when Mickey had waited for him the evening he'd been chucked from the football squad. Then it was dark; now it was light. Everything was light. Despite his weariness he almost felt he could run across the river. Fellows were speaking to him who had never noticed him before, calling him "Duke," men he didn't even know. In twos and threes they passed, turning to get another look. Yep, that man from the West who rooms with Mc-Guire, the varsity quarterback.

And all the way there was Mickey's cheery chatter. "Yessir, moment I saw you catch up with Whitney . . . when you got up there along-side Whitney I said to Fog, I said, Boy, this is a race, this is. He'll never let that bird Whitney get away from him. Never. And I'd figured Whit-ney sure for second place. Then when you left him behind; kid, it was just as if you'd hopped a straight eight and he was on foot. What a kick you packed in that sprint! Duke, I'll never forget it, never. Say! How 'bout your dad? Your father. He'll be pleased, won't he?"

The Duke hadn't forgotten his father. Right at that moment as he was hobbling across the bridge watching the sunshine on the oars of the shells along the river, he knew his father was calling up the *Courier* office and asking old Mr. Swann whether they had any news from Cambridge on the Harvard-Yale meet. This was the day of the Big Ten meet at Ann Arbor. Imagine the *Courier* bothering with Harvard and Yale. But Dad would be anxious to know. He'd better wire. Say he had won and let it go at that. The breaking of the record would come out when Dad read the Chicago papers tomorrow. Yes, it would surely be in all the Chicago papers.

When he climbed the stairs and came in, it was the same sunswept room as before. Yet it wasn't. Then he was an outsider; a friend of Mickey's and Fog's, nothing more, a man who roomed in Dunster H 35. Now he had arrived. He was important for himself. Of course that meant the Circle. You couldn't keep a man out of the Circle who had made his H and just broken a Harvard record. It took three years, but he'd arrived.

An hour later they walked together into the Dunster dining room, all three of them. It was a triumph. There was a tinkle of glassware tapped by knives and forks, because Dunster was proud to possess the man of the hour. Everyone all over the room called at him. From every side they shouted his name, reached out to pat him or shake his hand. They even spoke to Mickey. "Where have you been hiding that colt of yours, McGuire?" And McGuire, prouder even than the Duke, called back over his shoulder. He was as happy as anyone. Almost, that is, because now the Duke had arrived. He was sure of the Circle at last.

After dinner Fog decided on a show in town. A burlesque show. They would all go in together. Instantly everyone sitting about the Common Room decided they also wanted to be included, so Fog went to the telephone. Let's see, six, eight, twelve, sixteen—say, a whole row. Down front. Could Fog manage that on a Saturday night? Certainly. Fog could manage anything. He rolled into the telephone booth and emerged in five minutes smiling.

"The front row at the Howard. Now how many are there of us in all? If there are too many someone will have to stand."

They went out and piled into the cars. Each driver seemed anxious to take the Duke. "Climb right in here, Duke." "We got room here for you, Duke." It warmed him. Made him realize that at last he really was one of them. In spite of them, too.

But when they finally got through the traffic jams and the lights and reached the theater, trouble developed. The front row was gone. It had been sold already. This disappointed the Duke. He had never sat in the front row of a theater before, and somehow it seemed a proper climax to the biggest day of his life. Fog's blond head could be seen inside the manager's office arguing that the ticket agency had sold him the front row and the front row he would have. Finally the perplexed and perspiring manager relented. How many of them were there?

They emerged from his office. "He's promised to put chairs down front for us," explained Fog. This was even better. They'd be closer to the stage. Together the crowd trooped down the aisle, while harassed ushers arranged hard-bottomed chairs just ahead of the first row, an arrangement which was not greeted with signs of delight by those already placed. At last they were seated, their chins on top of a big brass railing which separated them from the six-man orchestra.

One act was finishing in the confusion. The front row collected itself and gave the retiring performers a tremendous hand. The two dancers appeared at the sides to smile their thanks. They were lined and old, their makeup was overdone and splotchy on their faces. The Duke had never been so close to the stage before. It was an experience all right, but he was not certain he liked some things in the experience. But he soon forgot himself in the general noise all around.

The weary orchestra struck up a lively tune and from the wings danced a man dressed in checked trousers, a green coat, and a red bow tie, and a woman in a satin costume with a short skirt that once had been white. They came down center, their mouths moving but no sounds reaching even to the chairs of the undergraduates, for everyone was shouting. The couple finished their song of which no one heard a word, pattered to the wings, and with pathetic and meaningless gestures disappeared.

Out came the manager, perspiring still. The noise which had abated, grew to a roar, and after his first few words, "Please . . . give . . . the . . . perform . . . ." he, also, was talking without making sounds. He held up his hands for quiet, but the shouting merely increased. A mob spirit had the theater in its grip. Shaking his head he disappeared in the wings, and for a while the noise continued. Finally except for cries all over of "Get on with the show," there was comparative silence.

At last the curtain rose. "That manager-man is tricky," shouted Mickey to the Duke. The stage had been set for a group of trained seals who were placed on tubs in a semicircle round the floor. In the center stood their trainer dressed in high boots and a conventional circus costume, brandishing his whip. The roar and noise rose in volume, but whereas it could make singers and comedians look silly, the seals ignored it. The manager was tricky all right. Because the seals went placidly through their act, balancing balls, tossing them back and forth, and responding promptly to every crack of the trainer's whip. Slowly the noise died down. The seals had conquered the mob.

"Let's give them a hand, boys," said McGuire, and in unison the row of chairs cheered as a seal balanced a tub on his pointed nose. The danger was passing. Gradually the audience subsided and became normal.

If only Fog hadn't been eating peanuts. How was he to know seals loved peanuts? As the noise died away and the auditorium became quiet, the crack-crack-crack of his peanuts could be distinctly heard in the forepart of the stage. The smell, too, must have reached up there. All at once the seal nearest to the footlights on Fog's end of the house waved his glistening head. At every crack he turned toward Fog and Mickey. Observing this, Fog tossed up a peanut which the seal on his perch caught and crunched. Immediately the next seal flopped off his perch and waddled boldly down to the footlights, his absurd face waving in the air, his nose quivering like a dog's. Again Fog tossed a peanut. Instantly the whole front stage became a crowding mass of hungry seals, their pointed heads eagerly extended for something to eat. To the appeals, whipping, and shouts of the trainer they paid no attention. They had not eaten since the end of the performance of the previous night. The house again broke into noise.

How the cop got into it no one was quite sure afterward. He lumbered down the aisle just as the trainer, in despair at seeing the house get away from him, came down front and shook his whip menacingly at Fog. Someone behind them reached up, caught the end of the whip, and with a tug pulled it from his hand. The cop pushed his way forward and from the aisle pointed to the man to hand over the whip. Then he clambered over the front row and leaned toward the man. At this someone to the side reached across and struck him with a folded newspaper. The cop turned, and as he did so the man with the whip neatly flicked off his cap. He turned back in a rage. The whip had disappeared. He started to say something, when another well-folded newspaper cracked him on the head. All this time Fog was quietly tossing peanuts into the open mouths of the seals on the stage, and the trainer was running from side to side desperately calling for the manager.

The second blow made the cop lose control. Reaching out, he grabbed the man with the whip, and an undergraduate who was picking up the folded paper to whack him. Collaring them he started to work his way out to the aisle. Halfway along someone tripped him, and he fell into a squirming mass of students and spectators. The two men got away, and he rose blowing on his whistle. Mickey jumped on his chair looking for an exit. The whistle meant trouble. The crowd, now panic-stricken, was climbing over seats in an effort to get out. They were also running right into the hands of the Riot Squad which had already been called out by the manager.

"Duke. Hey, Duke! Quick." Mickey vaulted the brass rail into the orchestra, long since departed to safety.

A small doorway under the stage was locked.

"Nobody can go in there, Mister," yelled a voice from above. Mickey paid no attention, and with a kick of his leg sent it ajar. They stumbled into an empty and very smelly room, out the door and up a flight of stairs which led backstage. Then down a corridor to another door marked EXIT.

"Hey, youse guys. You can't go through there." He was a big stagehand. The house now was full of cops, the curtain was down. But here were a couple of the students who had caused all the trouble and he intended to make sure they didn't get away. So he rushed forward to intercept them, bearing toward Mickey who was in front and hardly formidable-looking in his street clothes. The two bodies met, but the Irishman was ready, and with a bodycheck sent him spinning to the floor. Down the corridor and up a flight of stairs they ran. The Duke's legs were poles of agony again as he tried to keep ahead of his roommate.

"Stop those guys," yelled the stagehand from behind.

An old man appeared in their path. "Look out, Father. Watch your step." McGuire pushed the old man out of the way and let the Duke by. "Beat it, kid. Get the subway, fast. I'll handle this baby." The Duke could hear the stagehand rushing after him, a couple of blows; then he was out in the darkness and up the side street to the corner. A police car full of patrolmen came clanging along. He heard someone say, "They've pinched a big bunch of students at the Howard." Just ahead was the subway entrance. He ran down, caught the first train that came along and hopped inside.

His face was wet and he was trembling. And his legs—how they ached. Let's see, only ten hours since lunch. Ten hours, and he'd won his H, broken a Harvard record, practically made the Circle, and almost been pinched in the Howard. That was enough for one day. He was going back to bed.

17

Had that stagehand been a football fan, the varsity captain-elect would have played no more. He would have been recognized and put on probation, if indeed he wasn't promptly fired from college. Because assault was the least that would have been charged against McGuire. Luckily the stagehand didn't follow sport. Or if he did in the confusion of the moment he failed to notice who his adversary was.

The Duke returned and wearily clambered into

bed. McGuire, somewhat the worse for his argument, followed half an hour later. Fog, of the three, was the only one taken to the station house. However, the sole evidence against him was half a bag of peanuts which merely brought him up on charges of disorderly conduct. Eventually he was released. The record of Dunster H 35 was safe.

That was Saturday evening. The Sunday newspapers were full of the riot, the raid, and the twenty-seven students arrested, with their names and an account of their college activities. Mickey and the Duke read this with more pleasure than Fog. However, nothing happened until three days later when McGuire came into the room in the afternoon.

"Well, boys, it's tonight."

"What's tonight, Mickey?" They assumed he referred to the riot.

"The Circle. They're coming up here this evening."

"How do you know?" They couldn't believe it. That marvelous man McGuire knew everything. Wherever did he get his information? He sat down and became mysterious. But he was certain enough of his facts. The Circle was out

195

that evening. And they were going to be chosen. A near thing, thought the Duke. One week earlier he had only been a man from the West who roomed with McGuire. Now he was Wellington the Iron Duke, the bird who broke the two-mile record and won the Yale meet, a certain scorer in the Intercollegiates. Naturally they couldn't pass him up—now. What a break. And what a break for his father. How pleased Dad would be. The Circle at last. Well, it showed that if only you stuck things out. He looked back over his freshman year to the despairing moments when he wanted to cut and run. When he would have cut and run but for Mickey and Fog, especially Mickey who had pulled him through. He leaned across.

"If I make the Circle, it's due to you, Mickey."

"Sure it is. I won that race Saturday from the stands. You're crazy."

Evening. The warm May night came in the open window as the three sat there in the darkness. The Duke was on the window seat, Fog in his armchair, and Mickey as usual with his feet on his desk. Things of this sort, they agreed, were better done at Cambridge. Down in New Haven they had a kind of public orgy called

"Tap Day" in which men were chosen from the assembled class. This business of coming privately to a man's room was an improvement. Funny, but seven days before all this would have been an unpleasant subject to the Duke. Now he didn't mind. The Circle was his at last.

Fog sat up. "What's that?"

They listened. The Duke went back and opened the bedroom window. Far back toward the Square came an indistinct murmur, now rising, now falling, now rising again. Many times they had lain in bed and listened, but tonight the tune was full of meaning for them all. It was the song of the Circle, the song that they sang when they were choosing men. Weird, mysterious, yet irresistibly impressive, the rhythm floated into the room. Then it stopped. Only the roar of traffic from the Drive could be heard.

"Yep. It's them all right." The Duke's voice was husky. "They're in Plympton Street now. They ought to turn up Mt. Auburn. There they go. Bet they stop for Haines."

Haines, with Mickey, was the star football player of the class. They strained to listen. Nothing. Then it began again, louder and louder. No mistake, it was near enough to distinguish the hundreds of young voices rising and falling in the spring evening. Eerie and ghostlike, it drew closer to the darkened room where the three sat in tense attitudes of expectancy.

"Ohhh . . . oh . . . ohhh." Right in the rear of the building they were now. Now they were passing behind McKinlock and breaking through into the quadrangle. The head of the column trooped into the quadrangle, and the sound of their feet could be heard, the noise of the plaintive tune flooding the entire building. Outside the pounding of feet stopped. A door slammed below. Several pairs of feet came up two steps at a time.

Someone knocked furiously at the door. For once Mickey's throat was dry, he had no answer. Then the door flew open and there was an exclamation. A curse and fumbling for the lights. The Duke looked up to find Freddy Forrester and another man standing in the door, coats unbuttoned and shirts open without any ties. They also were dazzled by the illumination, and looked round for a second. Then without a word Freddy pulled Mickey from the chair, while the other yanked Fog out. Together the four stumbled into the hall and downstairs. There was a tremendous roar from below.

"McGuire! McGuire! Hey, McGuire."

The song began again. "Ohhh . . . oh . . . ohhh." Tramp . . . tramp . . . tramp. They were holding up traffic now as they crossed the Drive and went behind Eliot. Fainter and fainter. The Duke sat alone on the window seat. Beside him the curtains stirred uneasily in the breeze. An ancient hurdy-gurdy somewhere down De Wolfe Street ground out an antique tune. "Smoke . . . gets . . . in your eyes." It jangled and creaked as it played.

He rose and shut the door. Then he turned out the lights. Suddenly he realized he was tired; exhausted really by all the excitement and events of the previous week. He'd better go to bed.

The bedroom door was open and he stumbled in and fell on the bed. He couldn't bother to take his clothes off. He was tired. And—he had not been picked for the Circle.

18

"Wellington."

The Duke recognized the voice of the one man in college he didn't want to see. Ellis, the track coach, had a human sympathy toward people and he hated to let him down. But it couldn't be helped. Like his father, Ellis would be disappointed. There was just nothing to do. Well, that showdown had to come sooner or later.

"Hullo, Mr. Ellis."

"I've been up to your place three or four times. What seems to be the trouble?"

"Trouble? Nothing that I know about."

"What's happened then? Must be something up, you haven't been down to practice all week. I know I didn't want you to run on Monday or Tuesday after that race, but this is Friday. Did you understand? I sent one of the assistant managers up Wednesday and he couldn't find you."

"I was in the library. Reading period, you know."

"Yes, I know. But when you didn't show up yesterday I can tell you I was worried. Called up the Infirmary. Thought maybe you'd been hit by a car. Glad to see you're all right. How you feeling, boy?" He took his arm in a friendly way, for he was glad and made the Duke realize it. He was older, he was human, he might understand.

"Nope. I'm okay."

"That's fine. Fine. You be out this afternoon, won't you? No time to lose you know. I want to tighten up that sprint of yours, you were all over the shop coming up the backstretch there at the end. . . ."

"No, Mr. Ellis, I won't."

"Won't what?"

"I say I won't be out there running this afternoon."

The coach was puzzled. He stopped. This boy was normal and healthy, he'd just clipped three seconds off the two-mile record, won his H and beaten the most celebrated distance runner in the game. He was the sensation of the spring and now he declared he wouldn't run any more. They were standing near the steps of the Duke's entry, and men were passing in and out, eying the coach and his star runner with interest.

"Anyone up in your room now?"

"I don't believe so. Fog has an eleven o'clock and Mickey is usually out eating breakfast at this hour on Fridays."

"Let's go up."

They went up. The coach shut the door. These things could always be ironed out. Usually something troubling the boy if only you got to the bottom of it. "See here, Wellington, what's up? I knew there must be something wrong or you would have reported on Wednesday. You wouldn't let us down cold, would you?" He waited encouragingly, but the Duke didn't speak. It was difficult to explain, even to an older and understanding person like the track coach.

"If there's anything wrong, I'd like to know, any friction or anything. Thurber's a good boy, he sometimes gets hot when things don't go just right, but—"

"It isn't George Thurber. He hasn't anything to do with it."

"Good. I thought not. Why, he was as pleased last Saturday as if he'd been your father."

The Duke thought this unlikely, even allowing for George's exuberance. "H'm. You don't know my father."

"What I mean is, it couldn't be George—"

"Well, it is George." There! The Duke felt better.

"Why? What on earth has he done? I'm sure he's as upset as I am about your not showing up for practice. You know he has just set his heart on winning the Intercollegiates. What has he done? Tell me."

"Nothing. And everything. See, Mr. Ellis, it isn't George Thurber, it's all the George Thurbers in this place together. That's what makes it so terrible. They and their crowd. All the things they've built up and live for, the clubs and teams and papers and all the rest of it. Unreal, inconsequential, understand? And I've just—I had a shock last week which suddenly made me realize it. Suddenly, just like that.

Imagine, after living with them for three years. Pretty bright, I am, hey?"

The coach had seen a lot of different kinds, but here was a new one. He was impressed. "I think I understand," he said, not understanding in the least.

"No, sir, this place isn't Thurber or the rest of the Thurbers who run things. Or think they do. It's none of them or their activities, it's the great long line from—what was it—1636, down to the freshmen this year, each as important and no more so than the others, and all together making the thing we call Harvard. Some of those birds don't realize it. Never will. It's true, just the same. That's Harvard, not the trivial side-issues which seem so important that we fool round with here. Think maybe I told you last fall, I came here from the West to work. To get something out of the place. Now I'm beginning to. Guess I've grown up, sort of in a hurry. Running! What's that amount to? Another one of their side-issues. I ran and had a good time. It was fun. Because I won. If I'd lost it would have been awful. But that's that. I'm through."

For once the coach wasn't ready with the usual reply. This lad would take some handling. He looked out the window where a man in a shell skimmed over the calm water of the Charles. "But surely you aren't going to quit now. With the Intercollegiates coming along next week?"

"What do I care? Let Thurber worry. That's his baby. I've got my work to do and don't fool yourself, I get my kick from my work. Listen, I've just found a subject for my thesis next year and it's a honey. The tabloids, see? I'm going to work it up for a degree with honors in History, the whole story of the tabloids, how they started, why, how they developed and what they are leading to—it's romantic and exciting, and I'm interested. That's what I'm getting my kick from, not from having those birds call me 'Duke.' " He got up from the chair and went over to the window seat. "Honest, Mr. Ellis, it makes me sick. I can remember my freshman year when I used to go into the dining room of the Union and sit down at a table and half a dozen of them would come in and gang up at the other end as if I had leprosy. Would they speak or say good morning? Not a chance. I almost used to go back to my room and cry I was so darn lonely. Would have, probably, but for that roughneck McGuire, and Fog Smith, my other roommate. Nowadays

I go into the Commons downstairs and they won't let me eat. Those birds I was introduced to six times who still couldn't speak to me in the Yard are all calling me 'Duke.' 'Duke . . . would you care to play some squash this afternoon?' 'Duke, would you like to take in a show tonight?' Duke this and Duke that. Well, I wouldn't, see? I'm through with 'em. Now I know what I want. I want to get educated. I've had my fun and I'm finished. Finals coming in ten days. I must dig in. Maybe if I try hard I can get an education; that would be something worth working for."

The coach began to understand. He wasn't yet exactly certain what had happened, but he could imagine a few things. So he tried a new angle of attack.

"Boy, I certainly do sympathize with you. Yes, sir, I sure do. I know just how you feel. You come from somewhere in the Middle West, don't you? Iowa? That's right. Well, so did I. I'm not a graduate of this shop, I came from Kansas and then coached at Michigan and Penn before they brought me up here. I felt exactly the same as you. But don't let them get you down. You mustn't allow them to lick you."

"Lick me? If I go home next month with two

A's and two B's and a place on the Dean's List, how are they going to lick me?"

"What I mean is you mustn't let the place get under your skin. Now you just come down to the field this afternoon."

The Duke looked out the open window. He felt the gentle spring breeze, the soft sun. He knew the exquisite feeling of the springy cinders under his feet, the wind on his bare legs, the glorious sensation of opening his legs and lengthening out his stride, of drawing away, faster, faster.

"No."

Just that and nothing more. This baby, thought the coach, is sure a tough customer. When he said no, it sounded as though he meant it. As if more argument would only make him more firmly fixed in his determination not to run. He began to realize why that long-legged untrained colt won races. He also began to realize that anything was possible, even to losing an excellent chance to win the Intercollegiates.

"But look here. You can't quit like that. You're famous—"

"Yeah. So what? I'm famous, am I? Name the famous captain of the famous football team that beat Yale and Princeton my freshman year? That's not the kind of fame which means much—to me anyhow."

There was still one more line open. The coach tried it. "Seems to me, Wellington, your viewpoint is pretty sensible and I appreciate it. But don't you see it might be misunderstood from the outside. Ever think of that?"

"What do you mean?"

"You were an unknown runner two weeks ago, weren't you? Except to those of us down on the field who had been following your time trials all spring. I don't believe anyone knew you had it in you to do under nine-fifteen for the two miles. Even those of us who were sure of your ability weren't so sure of what you'd do in a meet. I've seen a lot of fast ones fold up in a meet. Didn't have the guts. Time trials and handicap races and class meets and all that are a lot different from meets with the boys from across the railroad tracks. All right. You go out against Painton. He has run one race that afternoon before he stacks up against you. Whereas you're fresh. He never heard of you and isn't expecting a real race. You run him off his feet, surprise him with that kick of yours at the end, and win. Now then. You're famous overnight. Suddenly you quit. You don't run again. See how it looks?"

"No, sorry I don't see."

"Why, folks will think you are afraid to give Painton another crack at you when he is fresh." In times past Ellis had used the fear motive, always with success. Invariably the boy on the other end would bridle up. He wasn't afraid. He'd show them! This time the attack sputtered and went out.

"Then they'll just simply have to think so. I doubt if you will. Or Mickey or Fog. Or my father." Ellis's face fell. He saw himself up against a proposition he had never met before. While he was wondering exactly how to proceed and what to say next, the door opened and Mickey entered the room.

Mickey was not surprised to see the coach there; he said nothing and neither did the Duke. His first real knowledge of the situation however came that evening when Fog was reading the *Transcript* in their room.

"So that's it, eh. Listen to this one, Mickey. Dorgan of the *Transcript* has this choice little item. 'Is it for scholastic or personal reasons that James H. (Duke) Wellington, Harvard's colorful distance find who ran Harry Painton of Yale into the ground and smashed a Harvard record in so doing last week, has dropped out of practice on Soldier's Field? The star two-miler was not working out this afternoon, and Coach Slips Ellis refused to comment on his absence. No information could be obtained about the likelihood of his starting in the two miles in the stadium next week. The Duke's retirement would mean the loss of the Intercollegiates, and heighten Cornell's chances.' Now, what do you make of all that?"

Mickey made a lot of things of it. He thought it was understandable, he thought it was regrettable, he thought probably it was a mistake, but most of all he thought it was the Duke's business. Sort of thing a man should decide for himself.

"We better keep out of it, Fog. Oh, boy, will things start to hum round this shop now!" The telephone rang. "That's things starting to hum right this minute."

Fog answered. "Hello. Mr. Wellington? Nope, he isn't here now. In the library, I think. No, I don't believe you could get hold of him by telephone there. Who is this? Who? Oh. Well, what do you want to know? No, I couldn't tell you.

So far as I know he'll run. His roommate. Yep, call about eleven . . ." He turned to Mickey. "Boston *Globe*. Sports department. Guess you were right. Things are starting to hum."

Things did hum. The life of the college which had passed the Duke by for three years, now whirled around his head. His action was called a ridiculous thing by part of the college. Another part said it was the only sensible thing to do under the circumstances. If he didn't enjoy running, Harvard put no pressure on a man to continue. The undergraduates forgot the imminence of examinations, forgot to discuss their favorite topic, the new president, and for one week everyone was concentrated on the Duke. The college was divided into two groups, those who considered he had a duty to run and those who considered he should do as he pleased. The first group was smaller but more articulate. It tried pressure of all sorts, none of it successful. It attempted to work through his two roommates, but Mickey and Fog were firm in their refusal to interfere. He ought to do what he thought best.

"Personally, Fog, I think it's a dirty trick of the Circle, and if he's sore I don't blame him. I know how he feels."

Fog was less certain. Wouldn't it be better

not to show them how he felt. To go on as if he didn't care. Mickey thought not. If a man didn't enjoy playing football he should quit. He would, at once. The Duke didn't want to get tied up with running. Well, that was his affair.

Then the *Crimson* appeared with an editorial on the subject. It was a real *Crimson* editorial in which for the first hundred words the writer explained the duty which the Duke owed to the coach and the team, and in the next hundred explained that Harvard was a place where a man did as he chose, and then ended with a couple of hundred words completely befuddling the reader who might wonder just where the *Crimson* stood in the matter. Right at this point, the Monday of the week of the Intercollegiates, Freddy Forrester came up to the room.

Forrester. Of all persons to send, Freddy Forrester, the president of the Circle. As the Duke saw Freddy's well-groomed figure in the armchair that afternoon, he remembered his visit to their room just after the Yale meet. This was going to be good.

"Hello, Wellington, how are you?"

"Pretty good, Forrester. What can I do for you?" It pleased the Duke to observe that Forrester was embarrassed and nervous. Freshman year it would have been the other way round. No one could say Harvard didn't teach you things.

"See, it's like this, Wellington. I just ran up to say that . . . I . . . that we . . . the Circle that is . . . feel they've made a mistake."

The Duke was surprised. He was surprised and he was interested, but he was not especially pleased. If he didn't exactly understand the maneuver at once, he was entirely assured something was coming.

"Oh, yes?" he replied noncommittally.

"Quite. We all want you to know how we feel. In fact, we've called a special meeting for next Saturday when we expect to take in one or two more candidates, men we've made a mistake on. Understand?"

"I see. Next Saturday, huh. Do you make many mistakes, Forrester?" The Duke wondered to himself whether his caller would have the nerve to come out openly requesting him to run. Or whether it would simply be assumed.

"Er . . . yes . . . why, no, that is. Not many." Forrester was uncertain about handling this bird; but on the whole he was encouraged. They had told him the Duke was hard-boiled. Really the man wasn't so difficult, merely a question of being tactful. Freddy rather prided himself on his tact. After all, everyone wanted to make the Circle, didn't they? Naturally. So you had a pretty strong argument on your side. Of course. Very nice chap, this man Wellington, in his way. "Well, you see that's one thing about the Circle. The members, I mean. We always stand together."

"I don't believe I understand." This was the exact truth. The Duke didn't know what he was getting at by this clumsy allusion.

"What I mean to say is, about this meet on Saturday." Ah, there it was at last! "It's the first time since 1909 that we've had a chance to win. That's almost thirty years—"

"So I've been told," answered the Duke, in a tone that would immediately have warned his roommates. But Forrester felt he was making an impression and kept on.

"You see Thurber was president of the Circle last year. I'm president this year. It's always a junior who is president, until the middle of his senior year. Naturally, as captain of the track team, the Circle is awfully anxious to have him win. It means a lot to the Club, you understand?"

Yes, he understood. The Circle. Not a word about the other men on the team, the majority, who didn't happen to belong to the Circle. Or about Harvard. The Duke turned his back. He was suddenly red in the face and he didn't want Forrester to notice it, because he was bracing himself to take that fat oaf by the collar of his coat, conduct him to the door, hold him on the top step, and give him a kick that would bounce him off the first landing without a stop. And he was just ready to spring when a thought came. He collected himself as well as he could and turned round, though his face was still red with emotion.

"Yep. I understand. Sounds okay to me."

Forrester rose eagerly. This man was a cinch. "Good. That's fine. Then you will run Saturday, won't you?" His anxiety to make sure he had understood the Duke correctly was sickening.

"Certainly will. I'll run Saturday, and what's more I'll be down for practice in an hour."

"Oh, swell! That's great. I knew we could clear things up, you and I, if we could only get together. Glad to have had this talk. Well, I must push off. Be seeing you Saturday. And the best of luck in that race."

A funny bird, that man Wellington. Not much like the men Forrester had gone to school with. No, not a bit, he explained to the committee of the Circle afterwards. Rather a dumb bunny, too. Fell hook, line, and sinker for the whole idea. Anything to get into the Circle. Yes, he wanted it badly, all right. But the curious thing was they'd parted good friends, yet the man hadn't shaken hands at the end. He'd just gone into his bedroom and slammed the door. A queer chap all right.

19

The Duke was watching Gus tape up his tender ankle when the coach came past.

"How you feel, boy?"

"Okay, I guess, Mr. Ellis. Wish the thing was over, that's all. This business of sitting round and waiting!"

"Yes. But that's what makes you a good runner. You feel things. The lads who take it in their stride don't come through in important moments. You'll be right up front there with Painton this afternoon. I know your kind."

The Duke shook his head. "Hope you aren't counting on my five points. Remember he ran two races against us in the Yale meet, and that was his third mile in one afternoon when he stepped out against me. He'll be fresh today."

"Maybe. Maybe not. We don't know whether he'll run the mile yet. Anyhow, don't go to the start this afternoon beaten. You haven't been licked yet since you began running and there's no reason why you should now. You'll find him tough if he's fresh. No question about it. If he beats you he beats you, that's all. You'll have the stuff next year to trim him, so don't worry. My guess is you can do it right now if you run your race correctly." He leaned over. "Watch Painton. That's all. He'll step out in front hoping you'll stay back in the ruck the way you did two weeks ago. That was a wonderful sprint you uncorked the last quarter, but he expects to be far ahead of you this afternoon—and maybe fresh, too. Understand? One race takes it out of a man's sprinting stamina."

"Okay, I'll keep right along with him. But just the same I wish you wouldn't count on my five points."

The coach didn't hear. Or refused to hear. He

moved off to speak to Davis, the hurdler, who was just going out for his qualifying semifinal. But the Duke knew the coach had heard, and it gave him a bad feeling in his stomach. They were counting on those five points to win the meet. Naturally, why not? Hadn't the coach said just that, way back at the start of college when he'd come up to their room with Whitney and Thurber? It was up to him. Everyone was always putting things up to him. The Yale meet was up to him. Now the Intercollegiates. Even his father had put it up to him; the Circle, for instance.

"Last call for the semifinals of the one twenty hurdles," came a shout. "First call for the mile."

The Duke went to the window. He stood watching the men troop out for the mile. When they had all gone over to the track, he leaned out and called to Mike, the doorman. "Did Painton go out for the mile? That Yale runner, Painton?" Mike hadn't seen him. Mike wasn't sure.

A couple of sprinters came in panting and exhausted. "How's it stand now?"

They recovered their breath. "We have eighteen. Cornell . . . sixteen . . . Penn twelve. Columbia . . . is up there. Yale's way back. . . . They'll save Painton for the two miles all right.

As long as they can't win. You've got to pull it off, Duke."

He dressed slowly and put his track suit on over his running clothes, because a cold wind was blowing outside. "Last call for the eight-eighty-yard run. Anyone up there for the eight-eighty-yard finals?" No, there were no Harvard qualifiers for the eight-eighty. The Duke took a blanket and curled up in a corner, the smell of turpentine and the rubbing solution from the tables across the hall striking his nostrils. This would be his last race, the final time he'd go through all this agony. No next year for him. Made you realize how folks felt before an operation. He'd heard his father and men at home talk about waiting for zero hour in the trenches. That's what it was like. If only it was over. He felt cold, and found he was shivering. The coach going past noticed it and put another blanket over his legs.

". . . And the bar in the pole is at twelve six . . ." said a voice underneath the window. "We have a chance all right with Wellington in the two miles."

Hang it, everyone expected him to win. Then the coach came back with Henry, one of the rubbers. "Start his circulation going a little. Duke, they tell me there's another bad actor in your event. Crouse of Cornell. He placed third to Painton last year and somebody said he had done nine twenty this spring. I understand Moakley expects a lot of him. Crouse and Painton; keep up with those two and you'll be all right. Get me?"

The Duke nodded. He had reached the point where he didn't care. Henry was slapping his legs and thighs, kneading the muscles of his back. Finally he felt better.

"Last call for the two twenty hurdles. First call for the two milers." The Duke jumped and tossed off the blankets.

"Take it easy. Take it easy, Mr. Wellington. You can stay here where it's warm for another five minutes yet. They won't start without you," urged the rubber. He had seen many nervous runners before. "You got all the time in the world. Take it easy. You'll get cold if you go out there on the field now."

But it was hard to take things easy when your heart was thump-thumping and you were as cold as ice, when you were so frightened. What was he frightened about? He tried to ask himself.

The race? No, the responsibility. The whole meet on his shoulders. For a minute he had the same bewildered feeling he used to have when he went into an examination, that feeling of confusion and helplessness. Then it passed. He regained some slight composure and stood up.

"Feel all right?"

He moved his legs up and down. They felt like lead. "Sure. I'm all right, thanks, Henry."

He went over to his locker and took out his shoes. The spikes had been specially sharpened. His last race. Only his second race, too! Several fellows spoke to him as he went out, wishing him good luck. Well, he'd need it all right.

On the steps he sat down and put on his shoes. A stream of strange faces in strange jerseys was going in and out. Men in blue, men in white and red, in orange and black, men with track suits bearing queer letters which he couldn't make out. He had a sinking feeling at the sight of this crowd. This meet wasn't the family affair the Yale meet had been. It was a contest of strangers. Painton felt almost like an old friend compared to these new faces. He jogged slowly along the edge of the track.

At the starting line he saw Whitney jumping

up and down, waiting for his name to be called. And Painton, too. So Painton was running the two miles. Of course he wanted revenge. The Yale man saw him, leaned over, smiled and held out his hand. Painton's hand was warm, whereas the Duke's was cold. He could see the crowd of starters who were gathered about the Clerk of the Course glancing curiously over at him. He was Wellington, the new Harvard distance man. He didn't enjoy their stares.

It was Whitney speaking. "Sure he's here. Duke! They're calling your name."

"Here." His voice was squeaky and high-pitched.

"Well, why don't you speak up when your name is called? What's the matter with you fellows, anyway?" The group turned toward him, grinning.

"Brown, Pittsburgh."

"Here."

"Crowley, Syracuse."

"Here."

"Meredith, Brown."

"Here."

"Stansworth, Princeton."

"Here."

He went on with the endless string of names. Seemed as if he would never finish. Gosh, what a gang. Then the Duke saw Mickey standing by the edge of the track. He beckoned and the Duke went over.

"Stay with them, old boy, I'll be right down here checking."

"How'd you get on the track, Mickey?" It was strictly against the rules for anyone not an official to be permitted inside the stadium during the meet.

"No. 49. No. 49. No. 49!" bellowed the Clerk of the Course. "No. 49, Wellington of Harvard."

The Duke hurried across the track. "I could disqualify you if I wanted to," growled the official. "Here's your place, fifth in the fourth row. Stay there, will you?"

The crowd tittered. He took the place assigned. This mob of runners was something new to the Duke, and terrifying. In the Yale meet there had been six men, here was a field of twenty-five or more to work through. And he was starting in the fourth row, which meant eighteen men ahead. He realized his inexperience, his lack of knowledge of race tactics. Fighting to the front through that crowd was a real job in itself. Even if there were no Painton of Yale up there in the second row.

"Ready now, you men." The starter stood beside them, his pistol over his head. The gang crouched down, and two or three in front leaned over on their hands the way sprinters do.

Bang! As the pistol went off and he started forward someone in the row behind gave him a push which sent him against the man ahead, who to protect himself shoved the Duke viciously with his elbow. For the first five yards he was fighting and struggling to keep from falling under those flashing spikes.

As he reached the first curve he heard Mickey's steadying voice. "Never mind that one, kid. Stay with them." He forgot his annoyance, and set out to fight for his place in the pack. It was a fight, too, and he was in a pack of wolves, all eager for the prey ahead. Already he could distinguish Painton's blond head several yards in front of them round the curve. The Yale man was running easily with that graceful and effortless stride for which he was famous. They turned into the backstretch, and obeying instructions the Duke decided to move up.

But it wasn't as easy to move up as all that.

He was the center of a shoving, fighting mass, and getting free meant elbow work and elbow work meant wasted energy needed later on. At last on the next curve he managed to drop back, step outside and work partly free. By this time he saw Painton and one other man well ahead. Coming down toward the starting line he heard Mickey and out of the corner of his eye saw his roommate's excited face.

"Get up, Duke, get up."

The bunch was more extended now and there were several small knots of men ahead; two Yale runners in dark blue, while after that were a couple of scattered men, and then in front Painton and another man, matching stride for stride, led the field. A white shirt with red on it. That must be Crouse of Cornell. Better catch those birds and soon.

He dug in and moved past a few struggling laggards. It heartened him to hear the roar from the stands when he passed them and reached the curve just behind the two Yale men. Trailing them round the bend he came into the straightaway determined to go past. From above they were shouting his name. He increased his pace, but so did the runners ahead. He moved to the outside of the track and one of the two moved over, also. Then he came back near the pole and tried to cut through, but there was no opening. Elbow to elbow the runners in blue kept going at a fast clip ahead.

It was a fast pace all right, yet those blue-birds were sticking it pretty well. Have to wait for the next curve and then work past. Painton and Crouse were up ahead, already there was a gap of fifteen yards and he knew this was just what he had been told not to allow. Pound, pound, pound, went the flying feet ahead. They were coming into the stretch by the start. There was Mickey—shouting something, bellowing at him, but he couldn't make out what it was. Too tired to concentrate on anything but running. Now for a good sprint to leave those devils behind.

But once more as he moved over on the track the Yale men moved over, too. That was it. They had him boxed. They were keeping him back until Painton had his lead secure. All the way up the stretch the shouts and yells urging him ahead continued, but as he tried to work his way past, they bunched together to prevent him. Of course he could shove them, but to do this meant a tumble, wrecking his chances, too. He could bring them all down, but they had no chance of winning and didn't care. He became furious as he saw himself hemmed in and unable to move ahead. Teamwork. That was the name for it in sport.

Then without warning the pace told. One of the Yale runners lost a stride, staggered and fell on the grass beside the track. The pace had cooked him. In the confusion the Duke saw an opening, darted through, and started after the flying figures up front. The stadium rose. That maneuver to keep him back had been plainly apparent from the stands.

Up front were the two leaders, further ahead than he had realized and going at a tight clip. Already the Duke's legs were aching, and his lungs hurt, but he knew this race was only half over. Could he stick? Would he last? Yes, but this was his final race, this was. Never again.

He came up the stretch to cheers of encouragement from the stands. What had started as a runaway began to show signs of being a real contest. At first he thought the cheering was for the man ahead, but words came down and once or twice he distinguished his own name through the coating of fatigue that was shutting him in like an anesthetic. The finish line flashed past and the ugly Clerk of the Course shouted at him.

"Three laps to go. Three to go. Three."

Three to go. And Painton twenty yards in the lead. He could see the Yale man looking over his shoulder as he took the turn in long, graceful strides. And Crouse. That boy was a runner. He was all the coach had said. Still up there with Painton. Two of them to catch. Gradually the Duke began overhauling the man in front. Whitney; good old Whitney. He went past him easily and set out for the two men in the lead.

Then a strange thing happened. Slowly at first and then faster, Crouse came back to him. The Duke, seeing this, increased his pace slightly and could soon hear the noise of his rival's feet. As he did so an answering roar came from the stands. Was he gaining? Yes, he was gaining. That panting, was it his? No, Crouse. Closer now, closer. He could see the tendons on the back of his neck standing out. Down the stretch they went like that, the other man just ahead, the Duke even, then Crouse a stride in front, until with an effort the Duke lengthened his stride and stepped out.

If only he hadn't been held back. His whole

frame ached, his mouth was dry, and foam was on his lips and drooling down to his chin, but his stride was strong and true as mechanically he forced himself to go out after Painton. More tiring, they all said, to run a front race as the Yale man had been doing. Well, no one could be more tired than he was. Charging up the straightaway he saw the blue jersey a few yards beyond.

"Go on, Duke, go on. Keep it up. You can . . ." Mickey by the side of the track. But the Duke didn't feel like going on. His mouth was parched, his legs were iron rods and every step meant pain. No, not pain, agony. He was suffering so much that the cheering and noise from the stands was confused and nebulous. There couldn't be much more, many more laps to go. There surely . . . couldn't be much more left. Down the stretch they went. Then the cinders from his rival's spikes spattered upon the Duke's bare legs. He could hardly see Painton through the haze of fatigue but those cinders were a signal. He was gaining.

Clang! Clang! Clang! The bell for the last lap.

Painton lengthened his lead. One more effort. Just one more, to hold him, to stay with him as long as possible. Ridiculous, of course, but he must make that effort. He dug in. He gained slowly, steadily, until he was right back of the Yale man. Then he dropped back and Painton took the curve ahead. They came into the stretch and the Duke made his try, his last, final try. All he had, everything. Elbow to elbow now, how long can I stand it. Half a lap. A few hundred yards.

Then he was ahead. He was ahead. The thought gave him courage. Head between shoulders, arms drawn back, he tore down the stretch. Suddenly there was pounding at his heels. Painton's sprint. The famous sprint. He could hear the pounding feet just behind him. Fifty yards, forty yards, thirty. If only he could hold those inches. The breath of the other man was on his back, gaining, coming up, now on his shoulder, now on the side of his face. Then it was back again on his shoulder. That way they fell across the finish.

20

The inside of her hands was dripping wet. She felt the handkerchief which for fifteen minutes she had been twisting and folding and rolling up in her palm. It was a wet linen rag. Well, the race was all over now. If only he hadn't killed himself. Statistics somewhere proved that athletes—what was it, burned themselves out. That they always died young.

". . . had a meteoric career, folks, because, believe it or not, this Iowa boy never ran before in his life until this spring when Coach Slips Ellis—and what a mentor that man is, folks— urged him to come out for the track team. He won his first race two weeks ago in the Harvard-Yale meet, but Painton had already run one fast mile at four-fifteen earlier the same afternoon, so everyone said it was a fluke, that victory. However . . . well, you all know what happened today and you heard about the Duke's magnificent battle here on this historic track in the Harvard Stadium . . . believe you me, folks, that was sure some race, hardly a sheet of paper between them at the finish. Now they're going off the field . . . that man beside the Duke is . . . I think it is . . . wait until I get my glasses . . . yes, that's his friend, Mickey McGuire, Harvard's star quarterback on one side of him there . . . the other man . . . the other man I can't figure out who the other man is from here . . . and there goes Painton right behind walking out with a friend and dragging his blue sweater on the ground . . . he looks all beaten . . . in fact both of 'em look beaten after that terrific duel . . . there, listen to the crowd give them a hand. Wait a minute. Here comes the official time, folks."

Mr. Wellington sat straight up in his chair.

Then he leaned over and fumbled nervously with the dials of the radio.

"Won by . . ." It was a voice from the official announcer over the loudspeaker system inside the stadium, but so penetrating that it came through plainly over the air. "Won by . . . James H. Wellington, Jr., Hahvud . . . second, Harry B. Painton, Yay-ull, third, . . ." Why on earth did they bother with all that. Who cared about third or fourth places? Had they broken a record? But the voice kept on. "Elmer F. Crouse, Cornell . . . fourth, . . . W. R. Whitney, Hahvud, fifth, Dudley P. Stansworth, Princeton . . . time . . ." But he couldn't continue. A wave of noise broke through the microphone. Back in Cambridge the crowd in the stadium knew instantly that a record had been approached, and that probably it had been broken. The announcer started again.

"Time . . . eight minutes, fifty-six and one-fifth seconds." Again the cheering broke in. It swelled and grew, louder and louder, wave upon wave. Mr. Wellington adjusted his glasses. He looked over at his wife on the davenport, and tried to smile. There was perspiration on her forehead. From where she was sitting she noticed his damp forehead, and realized that not only her boy, but the entire Wellington family, had been running that race in Cambridge.

"It's a record all right, Mother. It's a record. Hear them yell?" He tried to make his voice sound natural, but despite all he could do it vibrated with emotion. "Yes, sir, a new record, sure enough."

". . . making," continued the announcer, "a new intercollegiate record." The noise increased once more, then suddenly it was cut off as the control switched to the radio booth up top of the stadium.

"You probably heard the official announcer, folks, eight minutes, fifty-six and one-fifth; that breaks Don Lash's record by almost two seconds. Now I'm going to turn you over to George Davis down there on the field, who will try to get both contestants in this thrilling duel to say a word to you. All right, George, take it away."

"Hullo, everybody, we're right down here at the entrance of the stadium waiting for the two men to come across the field on their way to the lockers. And here comes Harry Painton, of Yale, that great runner who was just at Wellington's elbow in this thrilling race. Painton you know, was about a second inside Lash's record, too. Here he comes. Now, Mr. Painton, that was certainly a grand race, your last race of all, would you mind saying a few words to the radio audience?"

There was a pause of a few seconds. It seemed a long while. Then a panting voice which plainly evoked the struggle its owner had just endured, stammered into the microphone in a tone little above a whisper.

"Yeah . . . ran a great race . . . to finish second . . . what do you . . . have to do . . . to win in this league? . . ."

The announcer laughed. "Mr. Painton who busted Lash's record and yet finished second, wants to know what you have to do in this league to win. That's pretty good. Thanks, lots, Mr. Painton, and all good luck to you. Folks, that was Harry Painton, intercollegiate cross-country champion, captain of the Yale track team, who ran such a sterling race this afternoon in the two miles here in the Harvard Stadium. Now here comes the winner, Duke Wellington, who broke the two-mile record held by Don Lash of Indiana, and incidentally gave Harvard her first intercollegiate track meet since 1909. You remember the final score, folks. Harvard twenty-three and an eighth, Penn twenty-two, Cornell nineteen, Yale sixteen and three-eighths. He seems all in, this boy Wellington, he sure has given everything he's got, they're sort of helping him over to the field house, so I'll just ask him to say hullo to you." There was a delay. Then some blurring and scratching noises over the air, and finally the buttery voice of the announcer.

"Would you mind saying hullo to the radio audience, please, Mr. Wellington?"

Once again delay. Then a choked and muffled "Hullo." Mrs. Wellington twisted the wet handkerchief in her hands. His father leaned over toward the radio.

"And now, Duke, kindly tell the radio audience how it feels to be the new two-mile record holder." There was no answer. "Damn it all," said Mr. Wellington, "why don't they let the boy alone. Wish I was there."

The announcer cut in again. "This is Duke Wellington, folks, Harvard's new intercollegiate two-mile champion, who smashed the record held by Don Lash of Indiana this afternoon." He was stalling, and his voice became odiously persuasive.

"One thing more, Duke, then we'll let you go. Please tell the radio audience how it feels to be the two-mile champion."

Instead of the feeble tones of the champion, a strong Irish voice boomed over the air. People heard it in Boston, so did people in Waterloo, Iowa, and in Los Angeles.

"Get to hell out of the way with that thing of yours, big boy, or I'll bust you in the nose. Can't you see he's all in?"

Mr. Wellington roared with laughter. For the first time that afternoon, no, for the first time that day, the tension was lifted and he leaned back relaxed and amused.

"Wonderful," he said, snapping off the radio. "Wonderful. Mother, that must have been McGuire."

21

Freddy Forrester was pleased with himself. He had saved the day, saved it alone and single-handed. When everything seemed hopeless, when the Duke was stubbornly resisting the entreaties of men like Slips Ellis and Dick James, the president of the Student Council, it had been Freddy's belief he could arrange the affair. Freddy had immense and not misplaced confidence in Mr. Forrester. That was one reason he was head of the Circle. George Thurber had far less confidence. From some inside knowledge of the situation and the man, he had explained that Wellington was a queer lot. Seemed to have no friends in college except his two roommates. Whenever they were away he always ate alone at an outside table in Dunster House.

"Nope. We're licked, Freddy, we're licked. Nothing to do." But Freddy hadn't felt that way. He had been determined to have a try himself, because he felt certain he could persuade the Duke to run. "Sure, I remember him, I remember him perfectly from freshman year, though I haven't seen much of him since. He roomed in Lionel. Sure, I remember Wellington. I can handle those babies. Simply a bad case of inferiority complex, that's his trouble. Let me talk to him." Fred, old and wise in the ways of human nature, had never seen anyone refuse a chance to get into the Circle. Why should they? If you got into the Circle you were made. If not you were nobody. It meant a man's success or failure as an undergraduate. Absolutely. He had gone home and talked things over with his father who was a prominent trustee in Boston, and a man who thirty years before had himself been the president of the Circle. Like his son he knew a lot about human nature, and his opinion had coincided with Freddy's. Put the thing tactfully and the boy would agree. So Freddy had set out to do what everyone else had failed to do.

"Useless." So George Thurber believed. "A waste of time," was the verdict of Slips Ellis. "Pretty determined, I hardly think you'll get him to change his mind," said Dick James when he heard about the move. Even Mickey and Fog, drawn in and asked for advice on the best way to approach him, had allowed that if the Duke had said no, he meant no. They thought he would certainly stick by his decision. Naturally Fred had been slightly nervous when he found college opinion unanimously against him. But in the end there turned out to be nothing to it. Not a thing. It had taken him in all about fifteen minutes. No more. Proof that Freddy's knowledge of human nature and his understanding of the importance of the Circle upon the undergraduate mind was indeed profound.

So Freddy, taking a cocktail in the Pudding before dinner on the evening of the Intercollegiates, was pleased with himself. George Thurber, flushed with the wine of victory, agreed that Fred had every right to celebrate. They couldn't quite understand the reason for the Duke changing his mind, but Freddy explained. It was simple. "You see I went into the thing. You fellows all played about on the surface, you went at it superficially. Get the situation. Here's a man from some hick town in the West whose father was in the Circle. Obviously, this man wants to get in himself, more than anything else. Doesn't he? Naturally. He'll do anything to make the Circle. That's plain enough on the face of it, George, when you know the man's history and his background. Trouble is you fellows didn't go into it thoroughly. I just dropped round to his room and tactfully explained we'd made a mistake, and were going to take him in this evening. And he couldn't hardly wait to tell me he was going to run this afternoon. Why should he be interested in Slips Ellis or in you, George, or in Dick James? Or the others who tried to persuade him to change his mind? He wasn't interested in your trouble, he was wrapped up in his own problem. I found out what the matter was and solved his problem, that's all. You people had nothing to offer. Just a question of horse trading, that's all."

Accordingly Freddy that evening was in a happy state of mind. He explained the thing in some detail at least ten times between the finish of the meet and nine o'clock, when after dining well, he was ready to lead the Circle forth. After all, he had succeeded where other more important personages in university life had slipped up, he had saved the day and practically won the Intercollegiates for Harvard—the first time since 1909. Now he was generously keeping his word and giving the Duke his desired reward. Freddy, therefore, felt happy and virtuous. Because it would have been a simple matter to have called a meeting of the Executive Committee the previous evening and blackballed the Duke. That sort of thing had been done before, promises had been made and taken back. But Freddy kept his word.

So the column, Freddy at the head, swung triumphantly down Holyoke Street.

"Oh . . . ohh . . . ohhh . . ." A hundred voices in unison, a hundred pairs of feet going tramp-tramp, tramp-tramp on the pavement. The sound came in the open windows of Winthrop and Eliot and Dunster far down by the river, and men inside leaning over their books—Divisionals were beginning the next week—looked up and listened. The Circle was out again.

"Oh . . . ohh . . . ohhh . . ." Across Mt. Auburn they moved, stopping traffic, then down between Lowell House and the Athletic Building, Freddy stepping along briskly at their head, his shirt open at the neck, his head thrown back, singing lustily as only a man can sing when he has a clear conscience and has done a good deed for his world. He turned around, stepped out to one side, and watched the long line, six deep, arm locked into arm, singing the Circle song. It made him realize the tremendous power of united effort, the power that had conquered that stubborn Westerner when everyone who tried had only managed to stub their toes.

"Now then, you men back there. Close up in the rear." There wasn't any real need for closing up, but sheer exuberance of spirit made him assert his leadership. He wondered whether he was a born leader. Or were leaders made by force of personality? The column swung round the corner back of John Winthrop. Half a dozen windows in the house were open, and men in their shirtsleeves with pipes in their mouths leaned out to watch the line go past. Their rooms were alight, quite plainly they were not destined and never would be chosen for the Circle. Those who were to join the Circle never watched it before-hand, and when their time came they were warned and stayed inside their rooms, discreetly dark-ened. For a few seconds Freddy felt sorry for those men up there hanging out of the windows who would never know the unity and comrade-ship generated by the Circle. Never would they swing along, arm locked into arm, fiercely sing-ing the same song, down the same street, step in step together.

They turned sharply at Plympton Street, tramped across the green delta in front of McKinlock.

"Oh . . . ohhh . . . ohhhh . . ." chanted the line in unison. There was a soft perfume from the mist hanging over the river. It was, thought Freddy, an intoxicating night. Then they went into the inner court of Dunster, and gathered in a semicircle around the H entry. Freddy in-stantly took command.

"Thurber, George Thurber, you come along." A big figure worked its way up front and stood beside Freddy. They pushed open the entry door and went up the stone stairs. One flight. Two flights. There was the room and the card with their names on the door.

Joseph P. McGuire.
J. Faugeres Smith.
James H. Wellington, Jr.

Forrester pushed open the door. No lights. Just the way it was when he had come up for Fog and Mickey McGuire. So he reached round, fumbled along the wall for the switch, found it and snapped on the light. The room was empty.

Thurber, at his side, looked at him queerly, and he looked at Thurber. The crowd waiting below knew for whom they had come, knew who lived in that entry. The whole college knew it. Was it possible that he, Freddy, could have been mistaken? No. Try the bedroom. The bedroom door was closed. He was tired, of course, he was in there lying down. Forrester jumped across and threw open the door of the bedroom. It was as empty as the study.

22

It was the first week of June and the first hot day of the season. Mickey and Fog were walking down to Dunster together.

"Yeah. Remember how lost he was our freshman year back in Lionel? Gosh, that's a long while ago, Fog. He didn't know what it was all about."

"S'right, Mickey. Don't think I've ever seen anyone mature the way he has."

"Especially the last few weeks. He's grown

older right in the last few weeks. Have you noticed how his face has changed since those races?"

"Yes, all that took it out of him. Now the question is, what'll he do next season? With a year's experience and some more weight and stamina, he ought to make the Olympic team. Maybe this country'll have a real distance runner for a change."

"Hold on. Suppose he is made captain of the team next year. That always makes a big difference. Captains often do badly their last year. At least that's true of football."

"Captain! Say, I never thought of that."

"Why not? Who is there from our class? Townsend, of course. Ned Townsend, the hurdler, he won both his events against Yale—"

"And didn't place in the Intercollegiates. As I remember he knocked over a hurdle in the high and was sixth in the finals in the two-twenty."

"So he was. The Duke's about the only man from our class, isn't he? No, come to think of it, there's that fellow, what's his name now, Macomber. He placed pretty well up in the broad jump and got a third in the high jump. Then he's a sprinter. Seems to me he was second in the hundred against Yale."

"Macomber. I clean forgot about him. But he's just a good all-round athlete." They came into the court of Dunster and went up the entry stairs. "Duke has a college and Intercollegiate record behind him, and he could easily double in two events like the mile and the two-mile or the half and the mile in an ordinary meet." They stepped into the room. There at his desk was the subject of their conversation.

"Well! For Pete's sake!"

The Duke turned round in his chair. "Hullo, men."

"What are you doing here?"

"Working for that History exam. Where should I be?"

"It's twelve-thirty."

"What of it?"

"Don't you ever read the *Crimson?* Or hasn't your manager notified you—if he's like the football managers, he has all right. Meeting at the Varsity Club at twelve-thirty to elect a track captain for next year."

"Oh . . . that!"

"Well, aren't you going?"

"I hadn't planned to."

"Why not?"

"Not interested. Don't intend to run next year."

"What?" Mickey and Fog both stood still. "Not going to run! Why on earth not? What's biting you?"

The Duke leaned back in his chair. "Oh, a lot of reasons. I promised myself I'd show those birds what I could do. That I'd run the Yale race and quit. You know why I changed my mind and ran the Intercollegiates. Now I'm through. I did what I wanted and now I'm finished. Finished with Thurber and Forrester and all their gang."

Mickey slammed his books on the desk. "Wait a minute." He was red in the face. "Hold on now. When are you going to grow up? Just as I was thinking maybe you'd learned a little something since freshman year, you start acting like a freshman. Three years you've been round this shop and you talk as if Harvard was the Circle. Can't you get the Circle out of your head? Forrester and Thurber and their crowd, that's one small tiny part of this place. But they aren't Harvard. Any more than you are, you flat-headed Westerner—"

"Hey. I'm not a flat-headed—"

"Yes, you are, too, a flat-headed Westerner.

Don't you know those people aren't the whole place? Can't you ever get that through your thick block, stupid?" The Duke looked out the window. Wasn't that almost exactly what he had been trying to say to Slips Ellis a while back? It was true, too.

"Yes, Mickey, but a guy has, well, I don't exactly know how to say it, but a guy has a duty to himself. Here in this place a man does what he wants to. If he wants to run, he runs—"

"Sure, but there's another duty you have, my boy, and don't you forget it, either. You never ran until last season, did you? All right. Wouldn't have run then if Ellis hadn't heard about that crazy bet of yours and come up here and dragged you out onto Soldier's Field. Remember? That's right, isn't it? Now, this place is full of men like you: potential athletes, star football players, potential writers or actors or something else, only they get lost. No one pays any attention to them or encourages them. They're sunk—just like you were. Lost in this big world we call Harvard. Nobody is the least bit interested in them because everyone is so busy being interested in himself. But somebody ought to be interested in them. Somebody ought to get after them, pull them out of themselves and throw them into things, the way you were thrown in. Who's to do it but fellows like you who've been through it all? Huh?"

There was a silence in the room, a long silence. The Duke got up. "I'll run," he said. "I don't mind running. I like it, I suppose. Like to win, that is. But what's the use of my going up to that election? It's in the bag. Thurber's in the Circle. He's a buddy of Forrester and Forrester rooms with this man Townsend. They're both in the Circle, they come from the same school, both live in Boston—what's the use? It's all settled already."

"Can't take it, hey?"

He put his arm over his roommate's shoulder. "Well . . . you ought to know about that, Mickey."

"Sorry, Duke old boy. Forget that one. I take it all back."

"Look here," Fog interrupted. "Here's one thing. Did you ever think of this angle, Duke? If you don't show up there at the Varsity Club for the meeting, the Circle will probably swing the election. Because there won't be anyone against them. As I remember there's only a few Circle men on the team, but they're organized. They'll vote together. The rest of the crowd is unorganized. If you show up, it will sort of co-alesce the rest of the gang—they'll get together behind you."

"Right, Duke. They'll put up a fight if you appear. You're a natural for the job, only if you don't even show up they'll all think you really are sore. Now beat it, kid, and quick, too. It's a quarter to one."

The Duke shoved on his coat. "Okay, boss. You're right. That crowd is only a small part of this place. Thank goodness. Anyway, I'll run next year." He stopped at the door. "But say, what about Fog? Will he be able to stand it, will he be willing to live with us, Mickey? I should think one major sport's captain was about all the Dunster Funsters could stand."

"Attaboy, Duke. Go to it, kid."

23

The Duke hadn't written home since the race. How could he explain in writing to a man like his father who still thought of the Circle as the Circle? Times were different nowadays, but you couldn't expect him to understand a different point of view or realize that undergraduates had changed since his day. That being the son of a Circle man didn't mean anything in Cambridge, not even if you were the best man on the track team and held an Intercollegiate record. It didn't mean a thing if you didn't come to college with their crowd. Neither did it necessarily mean that you wanted to join yourself. That was going to be the hard point to get over to Father. He tried several times to say it in a letter but simply couldn't get it down.

So he just sent a telegram saying he was to leave the next Tuesday and would catch the nine o'clock train from Chicago on Wednesday. They'd know at home he should be at Waterloo about six in the afternoon. At last the final examination was finished and he was packed and sitting on the Wolverine westward bound. Mickey was due for another season of toughening in a lumber camp in the Northeast. Fog had a job in a New York advertising agency. For himself, the Duke felt he ought to be hardening up if he was ever going to make any kind of a showing at cross-country in the fall. Maybe he could get some kind of a railroad job; there were four roads into Waterloo and Dad knew all the station agents. You couldn't expect to sit at a desk for a couple of months and then be worth much over the hills in October. It wasn't the job which worried him, however. What bothered him was how to get things over to Father.

Ordinarily he'd be pretty excited about getting home. There were two or three boys he wanted especially to see: Bud Smith and Marshall, and then there was that girl who had moved up the summer before from Davenport. And certainly he was sick to death of college, of working for examinations, of tutors and conferences, of the library stacks, of the roar of traffic along the Drive, of that eternal roast beef au jus in the Dunster dining room, of the same faces day after day. Home food would taste pretty good, strawberry shortcake and vegetables that didn't come out of a can. If only it wasn't for his father. If only Dad hadn't made the Circle.

He changed at Chicago. Just after lunch they crossed the Mississippi and came into Dubuque. Iowa again. The familiar landscape was good to look on, and he was almost happy at being back once more. At seeing stations with names he knew, Manchester, Independence. About five in the afternoon the landmarks became recognizable. The train stopped at a small town a few miles out, and a minute later he heard someone calling his name.

"Well, Jim. Sure am glad to see you here, boy." It was Nick Devine, the *Courier* sportswriter. "Thought I'd run out ahead of the bunch and meet you. How are you? How's it feel to be a big shot, huh? Bet you're glad to be back just the same."

"Hullo, Nick. I certainly am glad to be back. Always good to be home again." Nick was unfolding a *Courier* open at the sports page. It was his picture in his track suit. "Hullo. What's all that about?"

"Just a small piece we ran about you this morning, Jim. I'm gonna do a longer story for tomorrow. That's what I hopped this rattler for. Want to know what you think about Lash, and do you think you can lower that record a few seconds next year, and what chances has America got in the Olympics, and . . ."

"Hey, there. Wait a minute." The Duke was gazing at his own picture, with the caption underneath.

HARVARD'S NEW TRACK CAPTAIN. WATERLOO BOY REACHES HOME TODAY.

It was all pretty sickening, all this sort of thing, but as Mickey often said, it was part of the game. You had to take the good with the bad, here and in Cambridge. He tossed the paper onto the seat opposite and answered the questions fired at him as well as he could. Yes, he sure would enjoy meeting Lash. No, he doubted whether he could beat him. Yes, he might clip a few seconds off the record, either of them might under good conditions. America's chances? He wouldn't know about that.

"Now let me ask you a question. How on earth did you know I was on this train, Nick?"

"Your dad told me. He sure is proud of you, Jim. Won't talk about anything else." The Duke flushed. Let him be pleased while he can, it won't be for long.

"How's Bud Smith? And Marshall? I hear Bud is football captain at State next year. Is that right? What sort of team will they have next season? Minnesota still pretty hot, aren't they?" Now the train was on the outskirts of town. He couldn't tell what he was saying. Waterloo! A darn good old place!

"Waterloo. Waterloo," called the conductor from the door. "Change for Des Moines, this train for Fort Dodge and Omaha." His voice faded away into the next car. Nick grabbed the Duke's bags, noticing with disapproval that they carried no stickers or emblems portraying their owner's fame. Not even a Harvard Track Team sign, he might just as well be a traveling salesman. However, he took the bags off the seat.

"Here. I'll take 'em, Nick."

"No, you won't. I don't often get a chance to carry bags for Intercollegiate champions. You go 'long." The train came slowly to a stop and the Duke climbed down. Instantly he was lost in a mob that rushed along the platform.

"There he is . . . there he is . . ."

Everyone was shaking his hands, a dozen, twenty people around him, patting him on the back, yelling in his ears, fighting with Nick to carry his suitcases. Boys he knew well, boys he had gone to school with years before, boys he hardly remembered at all, kids who had spurted into long trousers since he had left town, even one or two older men. Gosh, it was great to be back. The hometown. Where folks called you Jim. He was hurried across the platform and through the station into the outstretched arms of his father.

"Dad!"

"Jim! Well, well, boy."

There was a crowd about them. There was Mr.

Phillips, the high school principal. The old geezer loved to talk, just the same as ever. He was still full of big words and long-winded phrases—bumble-puppy, Mr. Kennison at Cambridge would have called it. Anyway it was pretty silly and confusing, with the cameramen from the *Courier* climbing on the top of the parked cars and shooting away at him. Wouldn't that old buzzard ever stop? Why, he could go on forever.

At last he was home. Home again. The same room, same pictures, the same clock, it seemed as if he'd never left. There was Mother, and even Spot beside her, tail going thump-thump, thump-thump. "Yeah, Spotty old boy, how you been, old fellow? Been good dog? Have you?" Yes, everything was the same. He leaned over and turned the dials of the radio.

". . . George Bassett and his Swing Boys will now play for you their own adaptation of that famous classic . . ." Yep, everything was the same. Only he had changed. He felt older than when he had left, ages older even than his father.

The telephone rang. "My goodness, that telephone's done nothing but ring, ring, ring ever since yesterday. I wish those people would let us alone." His mother went into the hall.

"No. You cannot." Her girl-tone. He looked over at his father and grinned and his father grinned back. "I say you cannot talk to him. Heaven's sakes, he's only just this minute come into the house, Mary. His father and I haven't had a chance to say hullo to him yet." She rang off abruptly and came back into the room. "Nowadays these girls are so they pester a boy all the time. We wouldn't have thought of calling up boys like that in my time." He listened, realizing that not so long ago she would have annoyed him by talking this way. Now he was only amused.

Once again the telephone rang. His father rose with an exclamation. "Hello. Oh, hello, Tom. Just back. That's right, just back this minute. Would he speak where? I don't know, I'm sure. I'll ask him—no, you better call him tomorrow. Right. Good-bye, Tom."

"Your father," said his mother, forming her words distinctly and speaking under her breath, "he's been so excited the past few weeks they say he just hasn't been any use at all down to the office. Going to the Station every day to pick up the New York newspapers—"

His father returned to the room. "Tom Sullivan. Wants you to talk at the Rotarians next week. I told him to call tomorrow. Now then, son." He sat down. "To think of it, think of your making a success like this at college. Well, well."

"But see here, Father." It had better come out now than later. Get it over with. "I'm not really a success, you know. I never made the Circle."

A puzzled look came over his father's face. "Eh? What's that? The Circle? Oh, yes, I forgot. Now, look here, Jim, don't go making any engagements for after supper when the telephone starts ringing. I want to hear about that race, from start to finish. And you'd better begin right this minute."

Turn the page to discover more exciting books in the Odyssey series.

Other books in the Odyssey series:

William O. Steele
☐ THE BUFFALO KNIFE
☐ FLAMING ARROWS
☐ THE PERILOUS ROAD
☐ WINTER DANGER

Edward Eager
☐ HALF MAGIC
☐ KNIGHT'S CASTLE
☐ MAGIC BY THE LAKE
☐ MAGIC OR NOT?
☐ SEVEN-DAY MAGIC
☐ THE TIME GARDEN
☐ THE WELL-WISHERS

Anne Holm
☐ NORTH TO FREEDOM

John R. Tunis
☐ IRON DUKE
☐ THE DUKE DECIDES
☐ CHAMPION'S CHOICE
☐ THE KID FROM TOMKINSVILLE
☐ WORLD SERIES
☐ KEYSTONE KIDS
☐ ROOKIE OF THE YEAR
☐ ALL-AMERICAN
☐ YEA! WILDCATS!
☐ A CITY FOR LINCOLN

Henry Winterfeld
☐ DETECTIVES IN TOGAS
☐ MYSTERY OF THE ROMAN RANSOM

Look for these titles and others in the Odyssey series in your local bookstore.

Or send payment in the form of a check or money order to: HBJ (Operator J), 465 S. Lincoln Drive, Troy, Missouri 63379.

Or call: 1-800-543-1918 (ask for Operator J).

☐ I've enclosed my check payable to Harcourt Brace Jovanovich.

Charge my: ☐ Visa ☐ MasterCard
☐ American Express.

Card Expiration Date

Card #

Signature

Name

Address

City   State   Zip

Please send me _____ copy/copies @ $3.95 each.

($3.95 x no. of copies) $ _____

Subtotal $ _____

Your state sales tax   + $ _____

Shipping and handling   + $ _____
($1.50 x no. of copies)

Total $ _____

PRICES SUBJECT TO CHANGE